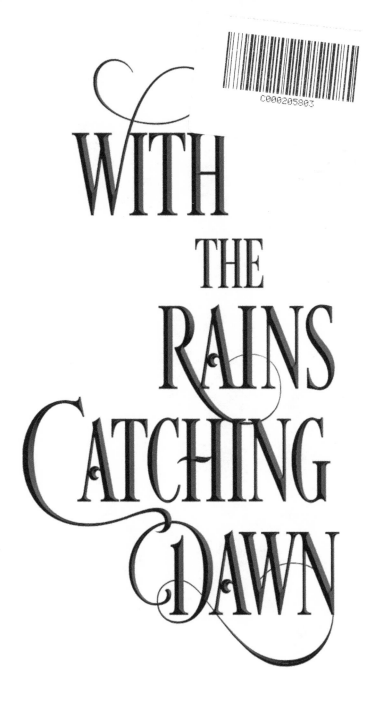

WITH
THE
RAINS
CATCHING
DAWN

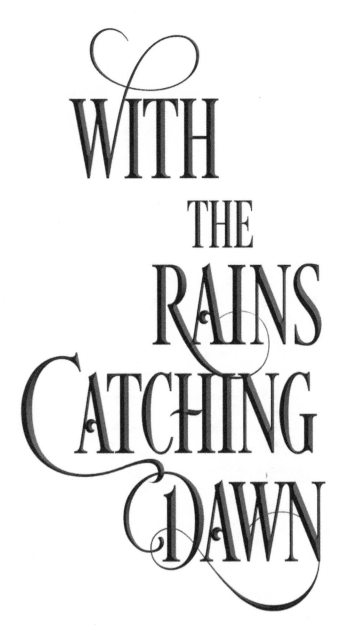

WITH THE RAINS CATCHING DAWN

NELLY ALIKYAN

WITH THE RAINS CATCHING DAWN

Published by Innocent Sinner Publishing LLC

Find me:

https://nellyalikyan.com

Copyediting: Ellie [https://mybrotherseditor.co]

Cover Design : Maria Spada [https://www.mariaspada.com]

ISBN: 978-1-956847-05-5

First Edition: October 2022

10 9 8 7 6 5 4 3 2 1

To

ALSO BY NELLY ALIKYAN

ALSO BY N. ALIKYAN

Buttercup Baby

SOUNDTRACK

1. Runaway by We the Kings

2. Hold On by Chord Overstreet

3. Will Carry On by Arkadi Dumikyan & Melisa

4. I

5. F

6. S

1

ETEL

Rumor already had it that the servants despised her. Actually, not entirely a rumor. Etel knew they despised her. Not all of them, but the ones who had deigned to give her the time of day when she first arrived at the palace. The others were as kind to her as they would be to a stranger.

But the ones she had been friends with? They hated her.

They blamed her for her natural gift of understanding the remedies that came from herbs, the lands, and the rains that befall their world.

They blamed her for moving up to a suite where she held her workstations in the front room and her bedroom behind a door. The suite was a modest living space in the world of palaces, but for a servant, it was a high luxury.

And Etel loved her little home.

But everyone else despised her for it. Even the servants she had no problems with. She could see they were jealous. Though it pained Etel to see it, she could understand it.

She'd only ever been happy for the servants who had been promoted before she'd become Remedies Expert, but Etel knew most didn't see it that way. For most servants, the promotion of one of them was a smack in the face to the rest of them. What Etel didn't think they understood was that she and every other one of the promoted servants had earned their way up. She knew she deserved it, yet felt guilty about enjoying the small luxuries the promotion came with.

She knew those old friends of hers would never understand, so she did not bother attempting to reason with them. They hated her.

It was for that reason specifically that Etel found herself enjoying her walks along the greens, even late at night. She made sure to carry a pouch of herbs on her person lest she need it for her own protection—a mix of spices that would burn an attacker's eyes completely—but in all the months she'd been on these walks, she'd yet to need it.

Or yet to be noticed.

The guards around the palace greeted her with a nod of the head in passing, but that was the extent of recognition Etel normally got from anyone at the palace.

And she was glad for it. The last thing she needed was the servants hating her even more because a guard fancied her or gave her any sort of attention, even if completely platonic. She knew that would only make their assaults worse.

The night was reaching the late midnight hour when Etel began heading back to the palace, knowing she'd steal away an apple from the tree harboring the kitchens and run off to her rooms on the second floor.

Another great part of her suite—it was on the second floor. Two above the lower levels of the other servants. Because she was no longer considered a servant, and that ticked off just about all her old peers.

"Etel!"

She stopped dead in her tracks, her heart picking up. Not

out of fear, but rather of shock. No one ever called to her. Or used her name. Even the servants who knew it called her other names.

But worse of all was hearing the name from Tristan, the Master Assassin's left-hand man.

"Etel," he called again as she pushed herself to turn to him.

He was jogging to her from the dungeons building. Etel had heard they had someone down there, that the Master Assassin had dealt a visit to Nuhmed for the man, and she could only wonder what he'd done to deserve it.

"I'm glad I caught you." Tristan smiled down at her in what was more a formal rather than friendly manner. "Would you mind running this to Sparrow?" He handed her a letter.

Etel barely felt it as her hand reached out to grab for it. Her brows furrowed. "It isn't sealed."

His lip twitched up on one side. "I'll trust you not to peek."

Etel was still caught on the fact that he'd known her name.

He nodded down to her like all the other guards on palace grounds and turned back for the dungeons before she could give a response.

She stared off after him until he was no longer in sight, then forced herself to turn around and head for the opposite side of the palace. The King's wing. The Master Assassin's suite.

The trip was short and Etel did a perfect job of blending into the walls so as not to bring to attention that she was headed for the King's wing. She knew she shouldn't care what the others thought of her since it'd always be negative, but she couldn't help it. It was a lonely world.

She was about five steps from the Master Assassin's suite's door when she heard a crash, along with a banging.

Another step brought her closer to the door where she heard the giggles of the woman the Master Assassin had surprisingly taken to his suite, the Princess's cousin. The Princess's perfect likeness of a cousin.

Another step and another little crash, the Master's growl this time. Deep and guttural and filled with the name of the woman within the suite. *Evony.*

Etel's cheeks lit up before she could control the reaction because though she may not have any personal experience in these matters, she had a feeling she knew exactly what was happening in there.

Etel rushed to the door then, knocking before anything else could be heard. She didn't want to interrupt the Master's *time* with his suite mate, but Sir Tristan had asked her to deliver this missive and she would do just that. Enough people hated her already. She wouldn't add the Master's left-hand man to the list.

It took a moment, but the door opened to a beautiful, giggling Evony.

A beautiful, giggling Evony who wore only the Master's shirt, whose hair was mussed, and who shined with a light sheen of sweat.

Behind her, a mess of papers on the ground was all Etel could see. Her cheeks burned as the image of their time presented itself into Etel's mind and didn't release. Because though she didn't have much to go off of, Etel had quite the imagination. She'd seen a couple of the married help enough times to know what the Master and Princess's cousin were doing in that suite.

Etel forced herself out of her thoughts and stuttered, "Is the Master here, miss?"

As if she hadn't just heard them. Her cheeks burned brighter yet.

Evony leaned against the door without a single ounce of

shame for what they'd been caught doing. Oh, to be so confident as her.

Sparrow moved for the door only a moment later, stopping just behind his missus in only a pair of trousers. Sweat also lightly tinted his skin, and hair mussed even more so than Evony's.

Etel couldn't help when her gaze latched on to the Master's chest—that chiseled body that came from hours of training and that speckling of hair—then jumped to Evony's shirt. Evony's bare legs to the Master's trousers. She couldn't help jumping back and forth and knowing they'd thrown on a single article of clothing so they could jump back into their activities after her interruption.

Etel wondered if she'd explode from embarrassment. She knew her cheeks were just about ready to as they blazed against her skin.

She forced her hand up to present the missive. "From Sir Tristan, Master."

The Master smiled at her lightly. "Thank you, Etel."

Etel made a small bow, then hurried on her way, ready to be far away from their room and her interruptions.

It was only when she was halfway down the palace that she realized he'd called her by her name. The Master Assassin knew her name. Though it shouldn't be shocking coming from him. He knew everything. It was part of his job.

And he *had* been the one to promote her.

Etel paused for a deep breath, then hurried along on her way once more. She hadn't been able to stop at the apple trees but knew there would be some for her to take in the kitchens. If she said she needed the apples for her remedies, the servants wouldn't be able to attempt to refuse her. Though they hardly ever did. Merely ignored her presence or mocked it.

Even worse was the fact that Etel was still burning from

what she'd heard in the King's wing. Because even though she had an imagination, she was a Northerner and unused to this outward show of intimacy, the uncaring nature in which they opened the door—most of the servants would be. She quite liked their boldness though, if she thought about it.

"No need to harvest the tomatoes, Jauc." Betti, the older of the servants who hated Etel, someone who had seemed almost grandmotherly to Etel before, laughed. "There's a bright, big one there."

Etel realized a moment too late that she'd stepped into the kitchen with the main group of six servants who hated her. The six with whom she'd used to laugh and cry with. Whom she used to be a friend to.

Then she was promoted as the Remedies Expert and they hadn't been pleased. It's when Etel had realized she'd never truly had friends, merely people who were good with her because they were all in the same station. True friends, she knew, would've been happy for her opportunities.

"I'm merely grabbing some apples," Etel responded meekly. She hated how weak she sounded around them but couldn't help it.

Etel had her hands on three apples when Stell's hand brushed her hair back the way she used to when Etel was upset, and for a moment, Etel was transported back to the time they had been friends.

"Aw, come, friend. What's got you so flushed?" Her tone mocked as her fingers dangled by Etel's hair, almost seductively. It was another one of the ways Stell teased her—she was the most *experienced* of this lot and loved flirting with Etel to make her uncomfortable.

Etel knew she was only mocking, yet answered for the slight chance she may be accepted, not as a friend, for she knew she could never find true friendship with these six, but as a peer. "I was sent to the King's wing to deliver a missive to the Assassin." She placed the three apples into a little sack, then looked up to the others. "I heard him and the Princess's cousin in his suite...enjoying each other. They were...hardly dressed."

There was no widening of eyes or shock or confusion or anything that would compare their reactions to Etel's. Rather, they seemed bored with the information and, at the same time, amused that Etel was so innocent that it had affected her so. Still, she knew the rumors would spread, if only to give them something to speak of.

Etel knew she was more innocent than the average servant. Knew that many of them found companionship with one another. But she also knew most of the servants held on to that Northern upbringing and were more reserved in their show of affections.

What she hadn't realized was that the information she'd given wouldn't shock this group in the slightest. She shouldn't have been surprised—Stell was one of the most experienced of all the servants, most of the others within this group not too far behind her. *They* were definitely the anomaly to the Northern born servants.

"*That* is it?" Betti snickered. "Child, everyone in the palace knows those two have been fucking each other's brains out since the moment she moved in. What? Did you think they were merely sharing a suite? That the Assassin would share his suite for any other reason?"

Etel could feel her skin heat up with more shamed embarrassment now.

Jauc, the only male of the group, threw his arm around Betti, but he was no closer to being friendly than the others had been. "Be kind, Bet. No one tries touching Little Expert. How is she to know?"

Stell picked an apple out of Etel's sack. "Not to mention,

those two aren't shy about showing their relationship. The way that girl holds him in public, I can vividly picture the way she fucks him. Kind of erotic. I touch myself some nights thinking of it."

Etel's eyes widened even though she knew she shouldn't be showing the others any reaction. She couldn't help it. They were Northern and she'd been naively sheltered from speech like this her entire life.

"Aw, Stell." Shawna laughed. "The girl will just erupt if you speak to her so. Don't you know she's more naive than a child about the pleasures of the body?" She quirked a brow in Etel's direction. "I guess to become an expert, you need to throw out the rest of your brain."

"C'mon, the lot of you." Again, Jauc made it sound like he'd defend Etel, but merely had his own ways of mocking her. "Give the girl a break. Some people just don't have the equipment. Or working knowledge of said equipment."

Etel cleared her throat, failing to recognize the way everyone stiffened before her. She reached for another apple from the bowl in the middle of the large kitchen island and threw it into her sack. "I must return to my rooms. You lot have a good night."

She turned and stumbled straight into a large chest.

Great, another one to ridicule me was all she could think before looking up to meet the eyes of the Master Assassin's right-hand man. Miels.

Those perfect dark green eyes, that hair that looked too soft to touch, and those delicious-looking lips.

Her heart jumped up to her throat, then plummeted to the ground. "Sir—"

"You lot aren't tired?" Miels interrupted her, not even acknowledging her presence but staring at the others behind her.

Etel didn't see them, but heard them stumble around and throw out their apologies to the man before her. Then the kitchen was empty. Eerily silent.

Etel took that as her cue to leave as well. She realized, again a moment too late, that though he'd been ignoring her presence, the question had been directed at her too. After all, he was still her superior.

Etel gave the slightest of curtsies, her head bent slightly, then moved around him.

She was stopped with a hand on her forearm, and again, her heart raced up and plummeted back down. Then raced with the excitement of being touched by *Miels*.

She met his gaze, worried she'd done something to add him to the list of people who despised her.

His eyes shined. Mischief and delight lining the edges.

At least that's what Etel thought. Those feelings had never before been directed toward her.

"Where do you think you're going, little one?"

2

MIELS

She was a small thing, barely reaching Miels's chest. And flushed so delightfully bright with innocent wide eyes staring up at him. Her throat bobbed distractedly and Miels found himself truly intrigued by a servant for the first time in his life.

"Sir?"

His cock stirred at the small word. *Sir*. So many people had called him it before. So many women. And never had he reacted so.

Miels took her in from head to toe. The nicer set of her clothes put her above the servants. So she wasn't one of them.

Then why would she allow them to speak to her like they had?

Unless she had been one of them. It wouldn't be the first time Sparrow had promoted within the castle.

She carried a small sack, which Miels had seen her throw apples into, over her shoulder, and her fingers fidgeted together under his scrutiny.

He narrowed his gaze on her, but every thought within him was based around wanting to know more about the little creature who allowed others to speak to her as if she were dirt. "Who are you, little one?"

Her throat bobbed again, then cleared.

Miels knew he had an effect on women, knew many of the servants would enjoy nothing more than to join him in his rooms. So he knew exactly what this one was thinking.

And still, he stood before her, waiting for the answer. Enjoying her jittery embarrassment.

She swallowed again. "The Remedies Expert. Sir."

His cock stirred again, but Miels ignored it and smirked. "The Remedies Expert?"

She nodded.

"Does the Remedies Expert not have a name?"

"Etel," she said so softly, Miels almost didn't catch it.

"Etel," Miels said, imagining moaning it while he touched himself that night. It *had* been a while since he'd had companionship, so he wouldn't chastise himself for the excitement of having a name for one night of playing with his cock.

She flushed deeper, a feat Miels hadn't expected possible, and gave a single nod. She looked like an animal braced for an attack, on edge, needing to run away.

Miels's lips twisted up, enjoying these reactions. "Do you not wonder about me?"

Her eyes narrowed in confusion as she spoke matter-of-factly. "Everyone knows who you are, sir."

He took a single, minuscule step forward and leaned down. "Then say my name, Etel."

Her breath hitched as she gazed up at him, those dark brown eyes yearning and confused all at once. "Miels."

His cock didn't stir this time. No. It fucking woke up and

jumped damn near out of his trousers. Because Miels could imagine her moaning his name now, and it was far more delightful than any noises he made. It would be what he thought of while he brought himself to orgasm that night.

"Good job, little creature."

Her eyes were already dark, but Miels could see how he affected her. He could see how much she liked that small praise. And again, his mind jumped to what he'd imagine in only a few minutes when he reached his rooms.

"There's no need," she muttered. "For praise. Knowledge of your name, of all things, would not deserve it."

He wore a genuine smile now. "No? And what would?"

She stared up at him, still flushed deep and obviously bashful, but she did not break his gaze. Rather, she matched it, almost like *she* was challenging *him*.

Miels held her gaze for the entire minute she took to analyze him. Enjoyed this little game with his little creature.

"Knowing you need to have a special apple glaze over a pastry with a cup of the most bitter of spiced coffees in the mornings *because* you're so wound up from not having companionship in your bed for over a month."

Now it was Miels's breath hitching. His eyes widening. In true, pure shock.

Etel's expression didn't change, but there was a bit of pride that shined in her eyes, obviously at getting this reaction out of him.

Miels stepped closer, leaning down until his breath hit her mouth as he spoke. "You're right. That surely deserves the praise."

He moved so that he could circle her still form.

He was by her side, almost pressed to her back, when his lips came a hairsbreadth away from touching her ear. "Tell me, Etel, my Remedies Expert"—he chuckled as her chest rose and fell faster and faster—"any other knowledge that would deserve praise?"

She licked her lips and though Miels knew it was to push herself out of nervousness to answer him, he couldn't help imagining it was for her desire to taste him.

"You favor wearing your darkest of green shirts because of the hidden pocket where you can stuff small candies."

Miels's heart jumped. This woman, this creature who'd suddenly made his life intriguing, knew something of him that even his best friends didn't. Because even Sparrow, the Master Assassin, didn't know *that*.

Miels licked his lips now, more in anticipation of what would come from her next than anything else. Then moved so he was flush against her back.

Her breath hitched, and he could see over her small stature how her chest moved quickly. Could see her eyes flutter closed and her head fall back ever so slightly.

He leaned into her opposite ear and allowed his lips to touch her skin this time. "Have you been watching me, *Etel*?"

Her breathing was becoming ragged. "All the servants watch. Especially the King's Posse."

He tsked three times slowly into her ear and cherished the way her head fell just the tiniest bit farther back and her tongue shot out to lick her lips. "I think you've been watching a little more closely, little one."

Miels wanted more than anything to press his erection into her back. To let her know how affected he was. But he wouldn't do it. He had rules about this stuff—no sleeping with the palace staff.

It had been an easy rule. Up until this moment, Miels hadn't even found himself with the need to flirt with any of the staff.

"Tell me," he teased down her throat, then back up to her

ear. "Have you watched the others so closely? Do you know so much about us all?"

She swallowed hard and gave the most infinitesimally small shake of her head.

Miels chuckled at her ear and loved the way her eyes closed and her jaw ground. "I want to hear you, Etel. Tell me who holds your attentions."

He needed to hear it. Needed to hear her say he was all she thought of. And he didn't know why.

"You," she whispered, the sound quivering in what was no doubt her anxieties of his reaction.

Miels moved again, circling around her and stopping once more before her. He wanted to push her against the wall and press himself against her. Wanted to hike up her skirts and fuck her right there.

"What about me, little Etel?"

She didn't look like she wanted to say it. Her cheeks burned, and it felt impossible that she could continue to do so without erupting.

And still, Miels delighted in being able to bring the reaction out of her. Because he knew it wasn't the embarrassment of feeling stupid here. It was merely the embarrassment of bashfulness.

But to Miels's surprise, she met his gaze with resolve. "I watch you closely. I know things about you that no one else has noticed." She swallowed and stepped back before Miels could say anything more. "Now, if you'll excuse me, Sir Miels, I must get to my rooms and prepare for the new day."

She was gone before Miels could react.

Instantly, Miels missed her presence.

He breathed deeply to control himself, then moved for the King's wing. For his room.

He needed to get his trousers off and wrap his hand around

his cock. He knew he wouldn't last long, knew he'd have to be careful with the noises he made so the others didn't hear him call out for the Remedies Expert.

But he didn't care.

He needed this.

3

MIELS

Three nights.

He'd gone three nights picturing Etel's flushed skin. Her wide eyes. That delicious looking tongue. Picturing the way she'd sound gasping out his name as he entered her.

Three nights he'd come to thoughts of her, been unable to touch himself without immediately jumping to her. Wasn't able to push her out of his thoughts as he stroked himself. Wasn't able to *not* touch himself from the constant thoughts of her, the constant erection that didn't seem to want to leave him.

Even in his trainings, as he had two men coming at him, all he'd been able to think of was how much he wanted to throw her against the mats and make her scream so loud, that meek little creature would become a fearsome thing to behold.

He was distracted in a way that apple glaze over a pastry or small candies couldn't help. In a way that only feeling the tightness of a woman's cunt wrapped around his cock could help.

It made him especially thankful for the news of Rosaelia's little outing.

He was angry—furious—to learn that the Princess whom he looked to as a little sister had gone into town on her own and almost been hurt. It sullied his stomach and wiped out any dirty thoughts he may have of Etel.

It made training easier as he wasn't distracted, too focused on the anger of what could have been had his new sister, Evony, not been there.

And he needed that concentration with Sparrow's anger among them. His Mastery made him a better fighter than all the rest of the guards at the palace, and his anger at Rosaelia made him lethal.

Miels knew Evony was protecting him and all the other guards from Sparrow. Knew that Sparrow's anger was too great to hold himself back and had the Master Magician not been around, he would not have joined them in trainings.

But Evony was around, sitting on the foams off to the side and looking wearily more tired with each passing fight. Miels could only wonder how much of the brunt of Sparrow's power her magic was taking on to leave all the guards unhurt. Alive.

Miels could see Sparrow continuing these fights all day. He knew he felt *that* type of anger.

But they only lasted a couple of hours. Enough for every group of five that went against Sparrow to get a few rounds in. None of them lasted very long, but all of them tried their hardest. He and Tristan remained fighting the longest, but even they were no match to the Master Assassin in such a feral mood. If nothing else, this was some of the best real-world training they could get.

It was all stopped when Evony finally broke the silence that only held the grunts of fighting by calling out for Sparrow. To

Miels's surprise, the assassin stopped instantly and moved right for the Magician.

He stopped between Evony's trouser-clad legs and leaned in to rest his forehead against hers, whispering what, Miels didn't know, but suspected were thanks for allowing him this chance to get the rage out.

The guards would only see the Master and the Princess's cousin in a public embrace, so shocking to their Northern upbringing, but they wouldn't understand the importance Evony played in Sparrow's life. They didn't understand that Sparrow had been a shell of a man before she came around. Miels did. Tristan did. They saw their friend blossom at any mention of the Magician, even when Mr. Grumpy tried hiding it.

"The anger wipe away your distraction today, brother?" Tristan tried to smile at him as the others ran off for their showers, food, and responsibilities.

"Distraction?" Miels quirked a brow at his brother even though he knew Tristan had picked up that he'd had something else on his mind the past couple of days. Had Evony not been around, Sparrow definitely would've picked it up.

Which brought Etel straight back to the forefront of his thoughts.

"What is it that's got you like this?" Tristan asked, lips tipping up in what was obviously a way to trick his mind into forgetting he was angry with Rosaelia.

Miels could tell him about the Remedies Expert. Tell him that he'd somehow never noticed the girl. He could mention that the little creature had captured his attention in a way he'd never experienced. He could do all that, but he wouldn't.

Miels never lied to his best friends, but there was something in this predicament that told him to keep it to himself. Maybe it was the fact that they'd all agreed that palace staff were off limits. Maybe it was knowing that palace staff were off limits for a reason—for the mere fact that a night of shagging one could lead to a whole load of problems.

Or maybe it was because little Etel intrigued him so much, Miels wanted to keep her for himself. He wanted to be the only one that noticed her the way he'd been noticing her for three nights. Wanted to be the only one Etel continued to notice.

He shouldn't want things like this.

But he did. Wanted it and found no problem in allowing it to be an unfollowed desire.

"Nothing," Miels muttered, bitterness at not being able to touch the Remedies Expert clear in his tone.

Tristan gave a light chuckle. "You sound like you need a release, mate." He took his own swig of water. "It *has* been a while since we've gone out whoring."

It had.

Over a month.

A fact Etel had known. Had observed and known.

Miels shrugged and began walking toward the King's wing. He, too, needed a wash.

"Why don't we go?" Tristan followed him. "I'm sure Spar wouldn't mind, especially considering it would make us less distracted. Make *you* less distracted."

Miels rolled his eyes and was close to agreeing. Close to telling his best friend that they'd go out for the night one of these days and find a few women to play with.

But he couldn't do it.

Because like the past three nights, a face came to the forefront of his thoughts. Her resolve as she'd stared up at him, telling him details she'd observed of him. Details no one else knew. Her voice as she'd said his name, called him sir.

It was impossible. He wasn't allowed to touch her.

And yet, the thought of touching anyone else sullied his

erection faster than anything had before. It was a frustrating ordeal.

"I can't," Miels simply said, refusing to look his friend in the eyes as they continued the walk to the washrooms.

"Not tonight." Tristan followed him down the King's wing corridor. "Any night this week."

Miels pushed into the men's washroom and still, refused to turn to his friend. "I know. I can't. Don't want to."

A bark of laughter echoed loud throughout the room as Tristan prepared for his own wash behind Miels. "Since when don't *you* want to?"

Miels grit his teeth, angry with himself for these impossible thoughts rather than with Tristan. "Since right now."

The water ran behind him, and Miels knew Tristan was turning to his shower. "Whatever you say, mate."

Miels squeezed his eyes shut. Squeezed with the desire to get little Etel out of his mind.

But closing his eyes only made the image of her more vivid, made picturing her against these walls clear. Made seeing himself tugging on her wet hair as he fucked her beneath these waters too desirable.

And it was all making him hard as a rock.

In the men's washroom, with Tristan only a few feet away.

Miels breathed out and made sure to keep his eyes open and his back to his friend as he readied his own wash.

4

MIELS

Miels could not blame Sparrow for missing dinner with the Magician. After seeing that scar, and knowing the feelings that Sparrow undoubtedly felt for her, Miels knew he wouldn't have been able to compose himself if he were in Sparrow's shoes. If that were his woman, he'd be an utter mess.

He was an utter mess at simply imagining Evony and Gemma in that situation. He couldn't fathom how defenseless Sparrow felt now to not be able to do a thing about it. Or how pained James must have felt when the girls had been taken. How it must have killed him to walk into those rooms to find the love of his life tied up and beaten.

It made Miels sick just thinking about it.

Then he had a vision of Etel.

Beautiful, tiny, ferocious Etel. His little creature. A vision of her hanging by her arms, her short frame too small for even her toes to graze the floor. Her beaten, and a dagger slashed through her abdomen to leave a large scar.

Pain sparked so strongly up his chest at the thought that he had to stop and rest against the wall. Miels bowed his head between his forearms on the palace wall and tried to calm himself, to remind himself that none of that had happened to Etel.

The fact that it had happened to Evony and Gemma, whom he looked to as sisters, made him angry still, but it was nowhere near the pain of anything happening to Etel. Why was that? Who was she to cause such a reaction out of him?

Is this how James felt when he was looking for them? Not knowing what had happened to his woman and sister?

Is this how Sparrow felt? Helpless to do anything because all of it had already happened to Evony?

He hated it.

And wanted completely to rid himself of the feeling. Especially since it all had to do with this Remedies Expert, a woman he didn't even know.

He'd fancied girls before, lusted for them certainly, but never had he been so distracted as this one little creature was doing to him. That was her true power—break down her prey to insanity before attacking.

When he could control his thoughts once more, Miels made sure to keep them far away from anything happening to Etel, then turned for the remedies room. He'd always known of the location, but had never spent the time to go himself. He regretted that now. The possibility of having met Etel sooner stung his chest, but he swallowed it back.

He had a woman he needed to see. Because the little vixen was clouding every one of his thoughts. Thoughts that had laughed at Sparrow for how distracted he'd become with Evony. Maybe this was his karma.

Miels moved with purpose and noticed subconsciously how the servants scurried out of his way and blended into the walls when he passed them. Did he look so ferocious as to garner that reaction? It normally wasn't one he got. They always respected his space, but never scurried.

He could imagine that's how scary he looked. He felt far past annoyed at the little Remedies Expert.

When he got to the narrow hall that housed the door to the remedies room, he felt an indiscernible part of himself settle. He was close to her now.

He didn't allow himself to acknowledge that reaction.

Instead, he moved with purpose to the room and pushed the door wide open without knocking.

There she was, his little creature. Crushing herbs in a mortar and pestle. It almost made him smile until he noticed the man standing beside her.

He was dressed in a guard's uniform and who Miels recognized as Serg, a man on the younger side of their guards.

From the way Serg's eyes widened as he looked up to Miels, his features were still unforgiving. Especially now as an emotion passed through him so intensely, he didn't know what to do with it. All he knew was that he had half a mind to throw Serg out the window off the end of this room.

"Sir Miels." Serg looked like he didn't know whether to bow or not as Etel's beautiful little face shot up to find him at her door.

"What are you doing here, Serg?" Miels barked without meaning to.

"I-I," he stuttered. "I was asking Miss Etel for a migraine remedy. I have chronic pains, sir."

Miels knew he should calm down, but it was much harder than he'd given Sparrow credit for in the past.

Instead, he moved for the work table as Etel watched him with furrowed brows. They furrowed deeper when Miels stopped between where she stood and where Serg stood a little too close for comfort. Miels stood taller to establish his place.

Serg's eyes widened again as he took the hint and backed up to the other side of the worktable, a bit of fear edging into his eyes.

Etel finally looked like she understood what was happening and began to work faster. She did so in silence until a small vial was filled with a light purple liquid.

She moved around the table to stand before Serg and Miels walked with her, placing his body too close to be misconstrued. The shy little creature surprised him by gritting her teeth in what Miels could only fathom to be annoyance. She didn't acknowledge him as Serg kept space between himself and the expert.

She handed the vial over. "Allow a drop into a glass of water any time you require the aid. But only when you require it. Do not make this a part of your daily intake."

Serg gave a slight bow as he took the vial. "Thank you, miss."

A low growl left Miels which made Serg's eyes bulge out and his stagger to the door quicken. Miels followed to close the door behind him.

As he turned with the shutting of the door, he faced a little Etel with her arms crossed before her chest.

A sexy little creature.

"What was that? People are going to talk!" she admonished the second the door was closed, that bashful part of her long gone as confused anger stormed her dark eyes.

Apparently the meek little creature from the other night wouldn't be making its appearance today. Miels liked this ferocious side.

A very sexy little creature.

"Serg doesn't gossip. And he especially won't about us. Don't worry. Your secrets are safer with him than the Posse."

He was actually one of the kids Miels especially favored. Until this moment, that is.

"What us? There is no us?" She genuinely looked confused, and all it did was make Miels want to kiss the furrow between her brows.

"Then why are you clouding all of my thoughts, little creature?"

Her eyes widened now and there was a hitch to her breath. "What?"

"You heard me. I cannot find myself able to think of anything else for more than a few minutes before you're back to torturing my imagination."

She moved back behind her worktable and began to clean it, distract herself, avoid his eyes. "I don't know what you're talking about."

"I'm talking about needing to touc—"

"Is there something I can help you with?" she interrupted with wide eyes before he could tell her how very badly he wanted to hike up her skirts.

He smirked. "No, Miss Etel. I just find myself at a disadvantage with you and I wish to correct that."

"What disadvantage is that, sir?"

Miels's cock hardened at her use of the word. It only ever happened with her. That word had meant nothing to him before she came around. "You know all my little secrets, my creature. I think it only fair I know some of yours."

She blanched. "What?"

Miels took a stool on the opposite side of the worktable. "I intend on watching you work, Etel."

"Why?" She stared at him with wide, beautiful eyes.

"I just told you." He smirked. "I wish to know you as you know me. Every little unconscious secret."

"Why?"

"Why do you watch me?"

A blush erupted on her cheeks and she focused her attention on her cleaning once more. She ignored his question, and when she was finished cleaning, said, "I have a few remedies I must make. You are free to watch me if you'd like."

He smirked, liking that she'd accepted his being there. "I wasn't asking permission, little creature."

Her cheeks pinked, but she said nothing more as she continued on her work.

Watching Etel work was more erotic to Miels than any seduction all the women he'd bedded had done. Leaving for dinner with the Posse had been torture and he'd made sure she knew it. He'd especially enjoyed that small smile she wore when she thought he wasn't paying attention. She liked that she was having an effect on him. And he liked that she truly believed he could ever *not* pay attention to her.

He planned on doing the same thing the next day. Except he would get her talking then, get every tiny detail of Etel out of her.

But he couldn't do that. They'd been sent word that a lord would be visiting them for the next week or so, and preparations had to be made. While the servants readied his quarters, Miels and Tristan went ahead on the travel path to make sure all was well. He'd been too exhausted when he'd gotten back to the palace to do anything but sleep.

But he'd still wanted to visit with Etel, if only for a few moments. It was only the late hour and the sign on her door that said she was available only for emergencies that stopped him.

This was an emergency to him, but he also knew she would be fast asleep and he did not wish to disturb her.

So it'd been almost two whole days by the time Miels was able to leave training and meals with the Posse to go to her.

Her door was open as she concentrated on her work and hummed lowly to herself. She was absolutely stunning.

Miels merely crossed his arms before his chest and leaned against the doorway to watch her. He could do so all day and not grow tired. This definitely had to be what Sparrow felt for Evony, and if so, he wasn't sure how much he liked it.

She wore a small smile as she worked, and Miels could imagine seeing her like this every day and not grow tired.

Then her head lifted softly with her humming and she caught sight of him and jumped. "You scared me!"

"You looked so beautiful. I didn't want to interrupt." He pushed off the door and moved to her.

She swallowed, blushed, and stepped back to indicate to him not to get closer.

He stayed back—against every fiber in his body—because this was about getting to know her, not yet to claim her.

"You're back."

"I would've been back yesterday, but we had preparations," he answered her non-question.

"You want to watch me again?"

"No, Etel." He smiled, loving that she wore her reactions all over her face. "We're going to talk today. I want to know every-thing about you."

"But..."

"And you'll learn everything about me in turn. All that you haven't already picked up, that is."

"Why?"

His smirk was seductive, but he couldn't help himself. "I don't think you're ready for that answer, little creature."

She didn't push him to give her an answer. She merely stood tall and pulled out her work tools. "If you intend on staying, I must insist you work."

He finally moved closer because he needed to. "Bossy too, little creature? I like it."

She sighed like she was trying to control her reactions. "Miels, please."

"And first name basis? I rather like the sound of mine off your lips."

Her eyes widened and she exclaimed, "Miel...Sir...please, stop!"

"Okay." He laughed and took a step back. "No more distractions. Just talking and work. Deal?"

She swallowed again and nodded. "Deal."

He turned to the table. "You will have to teach me, my expert. I've never worked with remedies or serums."

"I'd expected so," she said as she placed a few ingredients before them.

"Fiesty, bossy little creature," he whispered with amusement and loved the way her cheeks pinked.

"You'll start off simple." She ignored him. "Preparing ingredients. I need each of the bark cut into strips and every herb crushed separately," she said matter-of-factly, then surprised him with a teasing tone. "Can the big spy handle that?"

He knew his eyes shined as he looked down at her and he wanted nothing more than to taste those lips. "I think so, my expert."

She bit her lower lip—and everything in Miels knew she wasn't doing it to seduce but out of nervousness—and turned to her own work.

"What is it you wished to speak of?" She broke the silence that hadn't even had time to settle. He hoped it was out of the need to talk to him rather than anything else.

"I wish to start with you, little creature. Then, if we must, we may come to me," he teased. "But really, start at the beginning. Tell me about you."

She still didn't look convinced that he was truly interested as she assessed him, but she did not argue. Instead, she turned down to her work and began talking. "I was born in the middle of the land, by the east coasts. My father loved flowers and herbs. It's how I became so good with them. It's natural, I guess. In us. My mother was a seamstress. They died seven years ago, sickness took them both. They had been a bit older when they had me. I was fifteen and needed to figure out what I was going to do. All I knew was I couldn't stay in that house, so I sold it and used the money to travel toward the palace. I figured any work would be better than no work because eventually, my money would run out.

"I couldn't get work here back then, not much to give I think. So I worked at the estates of the rich for a few years, then worked with an apothecary for another year before coming here. I was with the servants for two years, then got promoted to the Remedies Expert after the Master Assassin noticed my knack for the herbs. That's pretty much me."

Miels smiled. "That is a pretty wrapped up history. Now, unwrap it and dig deeper." When those beautiful brows furrowed, he specified. "Tell me about your time with the apothecary."

A warm smile grew on her face, and Miels was glad to have picked that topic of conversation. "Albert! He's such a delightful old man. I still try to visit him when I can. He was the one that taught me how to really hone in my abilities. Oh, and he showed me this one serum that completely wipes away small stains, the tailors here *love* it. And another that helps women in their final stages of pregnancy. Oh, and another..."

5

ETEL

It'd been eight days since she'd bumped into the Master Assassin's right-hand man and felt him at her back, pressed to her ear as he whispered to her. Only eight days since she'd first heard her name on his lips and wished for nothing more than to taste those lips.

Half of those with his constant visits. Those constant visits that increased her already outrageous desire for him, so she'd begun keeping herself too busy when he wasn't around so she wasn't tempted to go off looking for him, looking to observe him like she'd done for some months now, even from a distance.

She was seeing plenty of him, and though she loved every second they were together, Etel wasn't sure what his motives were—was he simply bored, or possibly intrigued by her innocence? All she knew was that if not yet, he would become bored with her soon.

She still loved every second of being around him though. Loved his visits that were able to somewhat sate her desires for him, but she couldn't allow herself to get too close. It was the only thing she wanted and the last possible thing that would be good for her.

He didn't seem to mind when she narrowed her gaze on him or stood on the other side of the workstation. He always smiled and watched her with those twinkling green eyes.

He didn't do those things with palace staff.

It was something Etel had always respected about the men of the Posse—that they wouldn't allow drama within the palace, so they kept the releases they desired to moments outside the palace. Even farther than the closest village.

But he was doing those things with Etel. She didn't know why, but now those fantasies she'd been dreaming of for months regarding a certain blonde spy felt more real. Now, she'd heard him say her name, multiple times. Her need to touch him was growing dangerously unignorable.

Which meant she needed to keep herself too busy so that the desire would finally go away and she could go back to the quiet, private life she'd been living the past year.

It was the perfect plan.

One that especially came to fruition when, already on day eight, he didn't come to visit with her again. She assumed that was him growing tired of her. Understandably so. He was the delicious right-hand man to the Master Assassin and renowned whore. He had plenty of options and her meek little self wasn't the most desirable on the list.

She would have thought all that had she not received a missive from him, specially sealed.

The servant delivering it wasn't one of the ones who hated her, but even so, she hardly paid attention to Etel. She was so giddy whispering to herself about the recent news of the Master Assassin's betrothal that it hardly looked like she was paying attention to anything else around her.

It was the other big thing going on. The Master Assassin,

who had never before shown any interest in anyone, was betrothed to the woman he'd been sharing his suite with. Evony.

While some of the help thought it a tactical move on his part to marry the Princess's cousin, therefore ensuring his place with the crown, Etel knew it was a love match. She could see it by the way the two acted around one another. The way they looked at one another. The way he looked at her.

It was simply how Etel wished to be looked at. How she wished Miels to look at her.

Etel shook herself from such thoughts and turned back to the missive in hand. It read simply that Miels was in need of a few vials—within the list a mix of pain remedies and serums, and concoctions to sweeten his tea.

Etel rolled her eyes at that last request. He'd tasted a tea she'd made for him while he was helping her the day before and had insisted he would become dependent on it. The man sure had a sweet tooth.

It didn't surprise Etel that he needed these two dozen vials. As members of the Posse, they always carried a supply in their rooms in case the need presented itself.

What did surprise Etel was his specific instruction at the end of the missive—*I expect the Remedies Expert to deliver the vials herself. To ensure their safe arrival, of course.*

Etel could imagine the mischievous way his eyes shined and the wicked way his lips twisted up as he'd written that last part.

Though she didn't know why. It's not like he was truly interested in her.

Etel carefully concocted each of the vials he'd asked for and placed them on a silver tray. She balanced the tray in one hand as she closed the door to her rooms behind her, turning the sign that informed anyone who needed her that she was not around, and steadied her breathing.

She transferred the tray to both hands, then began the trek to the King's wing. To Miels's room.

Her heart raced with the anticipation of getting a peek into his suite. And for the umpteenth time that day, she chastised herself for the excitement.

She was before his door faster than she'd imagined it would've taken her.

Again, she forced herself to calm and steadied the tray against her ribs as she knocked on the door.

When he opened it, she nearly dropped the entire thing to the floor.

For he was shirtless.

Etel swallowed as her gaze latched on to that chiseled chest and the happy trail that went into hiding beneath his trousers. He was a gloriously made specimen, one too beautiful to be allowed to be called human.

She ogled him. Knew she was doing so and couldn't stop herself as her gaze latched on to the spot the happy trail went into hiding. His trousers covered him, and if Etel wasn't mistaken, a tent was beginning to form, when she finally forced her gaze to travel back up. As much as she wanted to see that tent, ogling his penis was far too much for Etel. She followed the hairs up his beautiful chest until she reached his face.

That handsome face with those dark green eyes fanned with those long lashes and thick eyebrows. That jaw that Etel had thought about licking on one too many occasions, and that fluff of hair atop his head.

It took her a moment to stop ogling him. When she did, she froze.

And blanched.

He was smirking, obviously enjoying catching her enjoying the view, but that wasn't what got Etel's attention.

It was the large bruise around his throat that her mind had skipped over in the desire to reach his eyes.

But she saw it now. Large black and blue blotches around his neck like he'd been strangled by...by...Etel didn't even know.

And again, she almost dropped her tray. "What happened?"

He opened the door wider and moved to invite her in.

Etel froze, her body taking an involuntary small step back, and cleared her throat. "You don't need to..."

"Come inside, Etel." His tone left no room for argument.

Etel pushed aside the elation of not only getting a glimpse of his suite, but of stepping within, and moved.

When he closed the door and leaned back into it, his arm wrapped around his chest as he examined her, she almost dropped the tray a third time. Which was all she needed to finally set the bloody thing down because he was too beautiful and she would definitely not be able to hold out a fourth time.

She cleared her throat again, flushing at the attention Miels gave her, then placed the tray on the small table before the couch. "Everything you requested plus two vials to help with digestion. I figure with all the pastries and candies, you may appreciate it."

She turned back to face him, only to come face to chest for the second time in a week. Except she was staring at his bare chest now and had to really push aside the desire to lean over and lick it.

She took a small step back and looked up, again unable to ignore the bruise around his throat.

He smirked as he watched her. "Sparrow didn't like a little joke I had about his...betrothed."

Etel blanched. "The Master Assassin did this to you?"

The Master Assassin never used his true strength on the undeserving. And most definitely never on his Posse.

Miels shrugged. "Last night. He doesn't like the idea of anyone touching what's his."

Etel swallowed and fought the disappointment that threatened to cripple her. Of course the little joke would've been Miels offering to please Evony in some way.

Miels stepped closer to her and forced Etel to step back again.

And again.

A final time pressed her against the wall.

"Is there a reason you look so upset, my little creature?"

She shook her head because this little crush she had didn't have to be known. And it most certainly wouldn't be his responsibility to watch what he said around her. He's always been open about sleeping around. A lowly maid's reaction wouldn't be the reason he stopped.

"I think I've told you that I'd like to hear your answers, Etel."

Etel forced her voice to steady and said, "I'm not upset."

He smiled down at her. "But you *are* a horrid liar."

She was breathing too hard and needed space away from him to be able to properly think.

But he caught her gaze pass his shoulder and his arms caged her in before she could move.

"Are you jealous, little creature?"

"Of what?" she strained to get out.

He leaned in so they shared breath. "That I may like to take Evony to my bed?"

She closed her eyes to wipe away the image that brought on, bit back on her lip to stop her whimper at how much she didn't like the sound of it, and pressed back into the wall to give herself the semblance of space. She couldn't help it, her reaction was too involuntary and sudden to control.

"Open your eyes, Etel."

She wanted to cry, but made herself comply. Pressed her tongue to the top of her mouth to keep her eyes from watering. And met his gaze.

He looked like he was having fun. "I like seeing you like this."

Again, her reaction was involuntary and too sudden to control as her knee hiked up into his groin.

And because of the suddenness—and the likelihood that he would've never expected it from her—he didn't block it.

She knew she should be afraid of the fact that she'd just hurt the Master Assassin's right-hand man, but she couldn't care enough as he whimpered and fell over her, his forehead falling to her shoulder. But his arms remained caging her in as he held himself up.

"You're an asshole." She shoved at him but he was damn near triple her size and didn't budge. "Get off of me!"

He didn't move his arms, but he did pull away from her so she had the tiniest bit of space again. "And you've got quite the power in that knee, little one," he grunted.

"Fuck off." She was shocked by the use of the curse, but didn't care. Her eyes were beginning to water, and she couldn't allow for that. She forced the tears away again. It was so much harder than she could've ever fathomed.

She pushed his arm aside and was actually moving away from his still recovering form when his hand wrapped around her bicep and shoved her into the wall. He still wore that ridiculously charming smile. "I like seeing you like this even more."

He caged her again, but she was past caring. Instead, she shoved at his chest. "What the hell is wrong with you?"

What the hell was wrong with her? She couldn't speak to the Master Assassin's right-hand man like that. He was part of the King's Posse and could have her killed for such a manner. Not to mention, he was a perfectly trained spy. He could easily kill her for it.

"I like that you're jealous." His hand moved from her bicep and lightly grazed her jaw. "I like that you want to be the only woman I think of taking to my bed."

She hated how much she loved hearing these words. Hated that he knew that was all she wanted. "Why?" she whimpered.

His hand cradled her jaw as his thumb played with her bottom lip. "Because I want to be the only man you think of taking to bed."

Etel's eyes widened so large, she was sure they'd jump off her face and roll away altogether. "What?"

"I haven't been able to get you out of my mind all week, my little creature." His fingers skimmed from her jaw down her throat, teasing her every inch. "Fuck, I picked that fight with Sparrow last night because I needed something to let the tension off after thinking about you with past lovers."

She was innocent, blushed too much, and was shy. But he still thought she had past lovers. She couldn't fault him that mistake. Most Northerners were bashful when it came to speaking of their intimate relations. Sex was easily had, but never spoken of—in a land where even public shows of affection was a shock, it wasn't altogether unreasonable for Miels to have thought the servants called her false names. To think she wasn't truly naive about the body's pleasures.

There was so much to pay attention to, but all that came out of Etel was, "But you don't know me."

Even with the past days of constant talking. They knew everything about one another and hardly knew one another all at once.

"I don't have to know you to know that I want to be the only man that comes inside you." His hand stopped at her chest, feeling it rise and fall with her uneven breathing. "To know that you want to be the only woman I've been inside."

Bitterness filled Etel again.

"Well, at least your wants have possibilities. Mine aren't possible. Who knows how many women you've been inside. Just because you do not finish in them doesn't make it any better, you know."

His gaze snapped to meet hers. "What?"

"You heard me."

He pushed the hand holding him against the wall to put some distance between them. "Are you telling me you've never been with a man?"

What if this puts him off? What if his words were merely that, words, and he truly wanted an experienced woman?

Etel didn't care. She wouldn't hide who she was. She just stared up at him defiantly.

"I told you I need to hear your answers, Etel." He sounded like he was straining against a deeper need.

Etel ground her jaw. "Yes, I'm saying I've never been with a man. Never been touched. Never even been kissed. Is that what you'd like to know? That the flushing little servant girl truly is as innocent as they say. As naive as a child?"

She pushed him away and moved for the door.

She made it three steps before he turned her around, and both hands cradled her face. He searched her gaze for a moment before breathing out. "That's exactly what I wanted to hear."

Then his lips were on hers.

Kissing her.

Miels was kissing her.

And she was kissing him back, alive in all her dreams.

Except this was far better than any dream she could've fathomed.

When he pulled away, she looked up at him with furrowed brows, but all he said was, "I'm sorry your wants aren't possible."

Then his lips were on hers again and this time, his tongue played with her lips, asking for entrance. A request she would never be strong enough to refuse.

Then he was really kissing her and Etel was in the heavens.

6

MIELS

Miels needed this night with his brothers. He was glad that Tristan had suggested it. He needed the distraction from thinking of his little expert.

Because he'd kissed her.

He'd been the only one ever to kiss her.

Those lips were his entirely. And if he allowed himself the chance, Miels could lose days thinking of kissing her, touching her, tasting all of her.

Tristan was at the kitchens grabbing drinks and snacks to meet in their private training room while Miels moved through the King's wing to the Master Assassin's door.

He paused for a moment when he heard a light moan pass through the walls. He shook himself out of it, knowing he must've imagined the sound since he, more than anyone, wanted to catch the Assassin and Magician in the act.

Miels moved the extra few steps to the door and had his hand raised to knock when he heard another moan followed by his brother's voice. "Don't stop..."

Miels's eyes widened as he smirked with pure delight. This couldn't truly be what he thought it was.

He stood there a few more moments before he heard Sparrow again, past Evony's moans. "That's right. You're almo—"

Miels had to bite down on his fist to stop from laughing. He was truly hearing this—his brother and the Magician were having some fun. And from the sounds of it, that brother of his was giving the pleasure. Good man.

"...doing so good...fuck, Evony, don't stop, ba—"

Miels shook his head, a wide grin on his face, as he prepared to leave the hall and meet Tristan alone.

Until he heard Evony cry out, "Sparrow, I'm gonna come."

Miels bit down even harder and pressed into the door, loving what he was hearing. He couldn't wait to see how angry Sparrow would get with him for listening in. As much as the Posse liked to joke that all could be heard, there was a need to be pressed against the wall or door of the room in order to truly hear anything, so that's exactly what Miels did.

All he heard after that were their moans and groans mixed in the air before Sparrow's name filled the space and Miels knew the Magician was coming.

Miels finally pushed off the door and headed on his way, unable to wipe the smirk off his face. Sparrow would surely kill him for listening in, but he couldn't care less.

He made the trip to the training room quickly in his distraction at thinking of how he would bring this up with his jealousy-prone brother.

"What's got you so happy?" Tristan brought him back. "And where's Spar?"

Miels's smirk grew. "Spar is currently giving our magician an orgasm or two."

Tristan smirked now too at realizing Miels had definitely heard them. "He truly will kill you, brother."

Miels shrugged. "The Magician will protect me."

They laughed as he fell onto the mats, a set of waters and a plate of grapes, breads, and cheeses between them.

Tristan laughed and scoffed at once. "I cannot believe Spar is actually falling."

"No one more worthy of his affections than the Magician."

"Agreed. The girl is going to make him so love-drunk, he won't be able to remain calm without her at his side. As a Master, it's probably not the safest of relationships."

They both laughed as Miels muttered, "Yes, yes. I imagine we will get a few more bruises out of the assassin in our life. He makes it so easy." And they were the only ones not afraid of Sparrow, thus able to tease him, push him to his boundaries.

Then another thought turned Miels serious. "Have you ever thought of it?"

"Spar falling?" Tristan quirked a brow like that was an odd question.

Miels smirked. "No. Falling. You falling."

Tristan shrugged as he brought a grape to his lips and stared out the open wall of the training room to the forests beyond and the moon high above. "A few times in the past, yeah. Recently, not so much. I must admit though, the way Gemma craves James has made me yearn for it a few too many times. You?"

Miels's head hung between his bent knees. "Never."

Until now.

Now, he had this little creature who had somehow garnered his attention, and Miels had no idea what he was doing. He was used to seducing women for a fun night. He had never wanted more than a release. Never needed to try in order for a woman to *know* he was interested.

He wanted far, far more from Etel.

He needed her to know how very interested he was. Needed her to see her worth. Miels wondered sometimes when he watched Sparrow with Evony if his brother felt this too— this desire for her body, but also her mind and soul. The way Sparrow had thrown Miels against the walls of this very room answered Miels's question for him—of course the man felt this desire. He was so obviously falling in love with the Magician, his feelings far outweighed anything Miels felt for Etel.

It was torture.

Tristan picked up his drink, then handed one to Miels and brought it up to cheers. "Lets hope we never have to experience it, brother. It seems to cause more trouble than it's worth."

Miels didn't know if that was true. It surely caused trouble —that was the torture part of this—but it was definitely worth it for every smile he got out of Etel, every second he got to spend with her.

"Cheers, brother."

H is little minx of a creature insisted he help when he was in her workstation, and Miels normally enjoyed doing so. Enjoyed watching her take action, watching her command him and move with such certainty. He was normally glad to be behind a table so his erection was hidden while they worked.

Not out of embarrassment—he certainly wanted her to see it, see what she did to him—but out of comfortability for her. She'd never done anything, and he didn't want her to think they had to do anything until she was ready.

But today was not one of the days he yearned to not do any work. He was out of training and his little expert had no remedies or serums that were immediately required. She was simply stocking up. He loved that she worked so hard, that she was cautious to keep a backlog of needed remedies, but at that moment, he hated the entire concept.

Miels closed the door of the workstation, remembering to turn the sign outside to indicate the Remedies Expert was closed to anything but emergencies.

"Miels!" she ridiculed from behind him. "What are you doing?"

He turned and fell into the door, the smirk wide on his features as he watched her. "You're so beautiful, my little creature."

He loved when that blush erupted across her features. It was erotic. And it was all his.

"Stop it, Miels!" She stared down at the herbs she was in the middle of bagging.

Miels chuckled as he pushed off the door and moved to her, pulling her hands off those herbs and wiping them clean before pinching her chin to look up at him. When their gazes met, he gave a genuine smile and began moving backward.

She tried to resist as he pulled her along with him, but he was so very much stronger than her.

When he reached the couch in the corner at the opposite end of the room, Miels let the back of his knees hit the cushion and fell into it. He brought Etel onto his lap as he did so and reveled in her laughs as she tried to push away.

"Miels, stop it! Someone might see!"

He hugged her closer. "I put up the emergencies sign."

Her eyes bulged but she didn't fight as his lips grazed hers.

"I think you've been working too hard and I'd much rather kiss you right now."

"Miel—" Her argument was interrupted by his lips on hers.

They'd kissed every chance they'd gotten since that first time. Miels hadn't been able to peel his lips off her for long periods of time. She tasted better than anything he'd ever had before, better than any candy or pastry. It was unfathomable.

Her mouth opened to let his tongue in and she pressed into him, her arms wrapping around his neck as her chest pressed into his. He loved how much she showed him she wanted this, even if she was too shy to say it most of the time.

"Miels." She tried to push away. "I should get back to wo..."

"Oh, no," he teased and pulled her in tighter. "Even if I'm not kissing you—which is a long shot with how good you taste —I want us relaxed, Etel. I want..."

A sudden noise from outside had her jumping before they heard a loud chorus of laughter followed by the sound of a high-pitched woman's voice saying, "Aw, look, princess isn't working. What a lazy yatter."

An older, feminine sound spoke next. "Hm, I don't know, Stell. The yatter made her way up. I wonder how she convinced them to that. Must have one mouth on her, but then I remember what a childish prude she is."

A male laugh came, but the sounds were passing too far for Miels to hear any more.

It didn't matter though, they'd had their effect. While they'd spoken, Miels had watched Etel's face burn, but instead of the cute bashfulness that came around him, this was of shame.

Miels took her face in his hands. "Talk to me, my creature."

She gave him a small smile, but it was nowhere near convincing. "About what?"

"Remember what I said about you being a horrid liar? Do not try to pass this off. Talk to me. Why are they especially vile to you? And more importantly, why do you allow it?"

She shrugged, but wouldn't meet his gaze. "It's nothing."

Miels sighed and watched her as she tried to push off of

him to return to her work. He hated how that small group had so drastically turned her mood.

His arms wrapped tighter around her waist and he pulled her close. "You're not getting away from me until you talk. And even then, it's a low shot."

She watched him indignantly, but he didn't budge. He wasn't kidding. If he had to sit there all week just to find out what was happening in that little head of hers, he would do it.

Finally, when she realized just how serious he was—and how very patient being a spy made him—she gave in. "They were the group that showed me the ropes around here when I got to the palace. They were never family, but I had truly believed them to be friends. I told them everything, upsetting and thrilling, and they always supported me. It is only in hindsight that I realize they were merely supportive because they thought me and my exciting news pathetic. When I cried to them, they were there for me. They wiped tears and made sure I knew I was better than the situation. Again, only in hindsight do I realize they found me childish and only treated me so. But..." She began playing with his shirt, staring down at her fingers as they picked invisible lint off the dark green he'd worn because she said it matched his eyes—and to store his candies. "But then I got promoted, and I realized how much they truly believed me a joke. Someone to amuse them with her naiveté and ignorance. I was so excited when the Master Assassin came to me about creating a position for me as the Remedies Expert, I ran straight for them that night to tell. I thought they'd be as excited as they had been on any other occasion, but even more so because nothing had ever been so exciting for me as this."

Miels brought her chin up so she'd look at him again. "A lot of servants grow angry when their peers advance without them. I take pride that most of ours don't feel such resentment, but it is normal, little creature."

She shrugged. "I know."

His brows furrowed. "Finish your story."

She stared into his dark-green orbs for long seconds before dropping her gaze back to her fingers on his shirt. "I told them all what had happened—that I'd be promoted come the next morning and I would have a suite with my room in the back and a workstation in front—and they became...angry. I...I'd never seen them so *vile*. They began chastising me and belittling my knowledge and insisting I must've gone behind their back and done *something* with one of you lot. When they saw how deeply I blushed"—a deep blush filled her cheeks at her self awareness—"they realized that I had always been honest about that fact—that I was innocent through and through. But they were vexed."

"And you allow them to continue speaking to you so because?"

She shrugged. "I guess I understand why they're angry. Who was I, truly, to have been awarded this position?"

Miels scoffed, forcing her to look at him. "Is that a joke? Who are you? Etel, you are *the* Remedies Expert. The only one we've ever had. Do you know what kind of honor it would be for Sparrow to create a position because of your precise skills? But fuck even that. These past days working with you have shown me, Etel. You are an expert. And that is deserving of more than you're even given here. Do not belittle yourself."

"I..."

He ground his teeth at her inability to say anything, to agree with him. "I'll have to see how very high these lot feel tomorrow."

"No!" she interrupted. "Please, Miels. No. Don't talk to them."

"They don't deserve to con—"

"Miels," she pleaded. "If you go to them, they'll only grow angrier with me. Currently, it is only words and I can live with that. The same way you do. But please, do not go to them. I cannot handle them turning the narrative into what they had thought originally." That she was sucking him off to get this spot.

Because if he showed such interest in her life, that is surely what would happen. The rumor that the Master Assassin had created a role for the servant that had sucked—and fucked—his brother off so well, Miels had become infatuated.

He sighed. "Fine." And only because he understood the fact that they would talk no matter what. He knew that even if he were to fire them, the rumors she was so afraid of would spread. As part of the Posse, no one would understand better than him.

"Thank y—"

"But they will find out about us, Etel. The palace will know," he insisted because that was one thing he was sure of.

She swallowed. "Just...allow them the meager happiness they get from those few words. They have little else to excite them and everyone deserves something that excites them."

Miels's lips quirked. "Yeah? And what excites you?"

Her smile—which she tried horribly to conceal—lifted. "Before, the opportunity to do my work and the possibility of making a better concoction."

He leaned in so their lips touched as he spoke. "And now?"

A sinister smirk grew on those delicious lips. "Now, I love seeing the way you attempt to cut a rutabaga."

He laughed as he kissed her. "Wicked, little creature."

7

MIELS

Alexei was a prime example of why Miels loved that he wasn't higher in these political roles—though most would argue that as a member of the King's Posse, he had the highest role behind the King, Princess, and Master.

But in true politics, lords ran their towns and villages and were considered the next in power after the royal family. And Miels and Tristan were easily forgotten by most of these lords.

It was in moments like these that Miels especially understood Evony's aversion to being considered a Princess alongside Rosaelia even though she absolutely was one. She was like him, like Tristan and Sparrow and Gemma and James. They didn't want the spotlight or the politics. Edmund and Rosaelia had been raised for those positions and had no say in their futures, but Miels could also see in them the natural rulers that could reign a land. The Northern Lands were lucky to have them.

Especially with morons like Alexei running their towns, they needed to be especially great rulers.

That meeting with Alexei where the man finally told them

his true intentions of visiting the palace—a truce with the Island Nation in order to allow a few sorcerers onto Northern land—proved Miels's point.

But it also finally gave him something to look into that wasn't related to the mystery of this rebellion—though it definitely could be if the Islanders truly were behind the plague beginning to fester in the northernmost parts of the Northern Lands. A sorcerer somehow sending the plague among their people would help them come onto these lands.

Being part of the Posse, Miels found it more important to remain at the palace than venture out to those towns. He most definitely didn't stay because the thought of leaving a certain little creature hurt too much to consider. That would be outrageous.

In any case, they had men scattered all throughout the lands and plenty of runners to send messages so while he waited for a few of their men to respond to his correspondence over looking into the plague, Miels found himself in the library.

He'd just finished telling Evony that she was staying at the palace, by Sparrow's side, no matter how useful she could be in this rebellion. Not because she was the Master Magician; not because she was an heir; not even because of how much he and Tristan adored her as a sister—and, in turn, Gemma and James as well—but solely because of Sparrow's happiness. The facts seemed to ease the little magician, so Miels was glad to have said them.

Now, she sat back reading her book, trying to be useful to this rebellion while he and Tristan turned to their own books— ones on plagues. He would have to remember to go to the infirmary at some point to speak with Ashtyn about these matters.

Or possibly to her rooms. Miels could already see Old Lady Arba blowing up if she was bypassed for the special healer.

But neither he nor Tristan would be going to said healer until they had anything to go off of. Information from their men up north would take a while, mostly because they would have to do their own investigations before they could get back with anything useful, and he and Tristan still had some studying to do themselves. It was why they were in the library —there were plenty of books on plagues that neither one of them had ever bothered with, but would now become quite acquainted with.

As Tristan flipped through a book on common sicknesses, learning the histories and if and when these common sicknesses had ever been plagues—so far in two occurrences the answer was yes—Miels looked through a book recounting all of the most deathly of plagues.

The way for every one of these most deadly was always potions from sorcerers or use of remedy-made concoctions applied by very powerful healers. And this world hadn't seen a Master Healer in hundreds of years.

But the thought of remedy-made concoctions brought his expert back to mind. He wondered as his eyes glazed over the words on the page what a friendship between her and Evony would look like. Would they become fast friends like Evony had with Ashtyn? Etel's softer personality made Miels think she and Gemma would make good friends. Easy friends.

If only the little expert allowed herself to believe she deserved friends in high stations. It still made him scoff that she didn't see how high a station she held, but he couldn't fault her that. She had been a servant for years before being promoted. It would take some time to unlearn that. And though she'd been the Remedies Expert for close to a year now, most of that time had gone with her truly believing her status was still with the servants. Miels's biggest goal would be to show her how superior she was, to him as well as the others around the palace.

But the thought still made him smile—Etel and Evony and Gemma. And possibly Ashtyn. It would be nice to see Rosaelia in that mix as well. Miels knew she would like to be closer to the girls even though it was difficult for her because of how sheltered she'd been to only their close companionship all these years.

His thoughts were cut off by the stare he could feel on his profile.

Without looking up from the page, Miels asked, "What is it, sister?"

"What's got you smiling like that?"

His gaze shot up and he gave her a seductive, teasing grin. "You sure you want privy to *my* thoughts, Evie?"

A wicked glint passed her eyes as she stared him down. "I *want* privy to what got you those bruises!"

He and Tristan laughed and Evony rolled her eyes at them again, the amused tug of her lips not hiding how much she enjoyed their company even when she was annoyed with them.

Being a spy meant he was trained to go unnoticed.

In a palace where everyone recognized him, sometimes Miels liked the ability to go unnoticed. He enjoyed sticking to the shadows and moving about the palace.

Sometimes he did so with no end in mind, only wandering aimlessly until he inevitably got bored or found something of interest to watch or listen in on. It was part of how they secured the safety within palace walls so well.

Other times, he moved in search of others. Any time they

had a suspicion or wanted to check some of the guests out, either he, Tristan, or Sparrow would blend into the shadows and follow said person around. Sometimes, all three of them blended and followed around different people.

Miels was definitely in the latter boat at the moment—he was after those servants that were spiteful toward Etel. He wouldn't do anything to them as promised, wouldn't even make himself known—which might be difficult if they begin speaking of Etel—but he needed to learn more about them.

He was currently following the only male of the group, Jauc, as he moved for the servants' sleeping quarters. The man was tall and lanky, probably in his lower thirties, dark cropped hair, and honestly, a great cook. Miels may not like the group, but he would not fault them any jobs well done.

Most of the servants were given specific beds when they arrived at the palace, but it wasn't uncommon for them to switch. So it didn't shock Miels that he followed Jauc to a servant's quarter where the entirety of the group who hated Etel resided. He pictured Etel had probably resided here as well.

Miels was in a crawl space above them in order to make him undetectable and give him the peace to listen in without having to worry whether someone might accidentally bump into him.

The servants' quarters were smaller suites that each housed eight evenly made smaller rooms, and a tight common space in the middle. Each of the rooms only big enough for a bed, an armoire, and a chair. It did not surprise Miels that they'd all chosen to share this quarter. It was the one closest to the doors that led out to the herb garden. Etel would've loved being so close to the space.

As Jauc greeted everyone and fell onto the couch in a tired lounge, Miels analyzed the others. Ini, a girl with dark cropped hair to her ears who seemed to be the closest to Etel's age at maybe a few years older, moved immediately to Jauc's lap, kissing at his neck and letting his hand slip beneath her dress. Though the skirts covered what they were doing, it still shocked Miels that they were doing it. He was no saint, but they were Northern after all—public displays weren't common. And especially not these types of displays. Kissing and embracing he understood, sexual pleasure by these Northerners shocked him.

It also made him realize that they'd been hiding more than their selfish selves with Etel around because there was no way she would've seen this and not known she was too different from them.

On the couch opposite them in the tight space sat Betti. The woman was so much older than the others, it shocked Miels that she spent all of her time around them. The greedy look in her eyes told Miels it was so she could reap any benefits by using them. Using people her own age made those benefits smaller as the younger had more time on them.

The woman was an older, plump woman with greyed hair, but her eyes showed she was not a nice person. Again, though, Miels would not fault her the work she did. She was a very good servant, loyal to the palace. Just because she wanted a higher station and didn't like Etel did not mean Miels would try to find fault in her abilities.

Walking laps around those couches was Stell, the one that had passed by Etel's suite the day before and made her flush with shame. An intense hatred for the woman spread throughout Miels too quickly for him to control.

The girl had long dark hair, but was plain otherwise. Nothing about her called to attention and Miels guessed that was the reason the girl was so bitter—she believed herself above everyone else, but no one else truly gave her the time of day.

They were the only ones in the room, the others either not there yet or already off to bed, and as Stell plopped down beside the horny duo, Miels could finally listen to conversation.

"Stop it, you two! You're making me jealous," Stell bit out to the two of them.

Jauc only smirked at her as Ini's tongue licked up the side of his neck and she gasped at whatever he was doing with his fingers beneath that skirt. "So go find someone to fuck, Stelly Belly. I hear Jon wants you."

She rolled her eyes. "Jon had me yesterday, and he was satisfactory at best."

He laughed as Ini bit down on the crook of his neck and shoulder to stop from screaming as she obviously came in front of her friends. "Try Earl. Word around the kitchens is he knows how to please."

Stell's eyes shined and it was obvious this Earl man would be her next conquest. "Hm, maybe. But what I'd really like is one of those whores in the Posse." She sighed as she leaned back. "Imagine falling pregnant with one of them. I'd be set for life."

The comment turned Miels's stomach. Both at the thought of touching her and the fact that she'd only want him or Tristan and their child for a 'set life.' No ambition, no drive.

And she wondered why Etel had risen and she remained a servant. Etel had passion. She loved those concoctions she made so much, Miels got her speaking of them whenever he could just to see her eyes light up. She had the drive to continue trying new remedies to make the ones she had better; she didn't merely sit back because they already had a remedy for something. Etel had purpose. This Stell girl had none of it.

Not to mention, Etel would have his child because she wanted a family with him. Not for a 'set life.'

"Not to mention, they probably know a thing or two about pleasing a woman," Betti added.

"Your fucks need advice, Bet," Jauc teased with a wicked grin. "I'm plenty good at pleasing women. Shall I help those poor fools so you can get your releases?"

"Please," Betti muttered as Ini turned Jauc to look at her with narrowed eyes.

"Plenty good at pleasing women, Jauc? If I find out you touched anyone else, I'll take those knives you covet so much in the kitchen and cut your hands off."

He bit down on his lower lip to hide his amusement—poorly so—as his hands wrapped around her waist and he ground his hips into her. "Never, In. My cock goes into your holes only. My hands are for you. My tongue is all yours. I'm all yours."

She turned to straddle him and ground her breasts into his face. "Good, you fucker."

"Keep talking to me like that, I'm going to expect that mouth wrapped around my cock for punishment."

Ini gave a wicked grin. "Dirty little fucker."

Jauc moved quickly, lifting Ini in his arms and moving for a door that undoubtedly led to his room. Or theirs. They could very well be sharing. At least this showed they were in a serious relationship and Miels did not have to think about Jauc ever trying with Etel. Ini didn't seem to show any extra rage toward the Remedies Expert, so Miels could safely assume Jauc had never lain interest.

Left with only Betti and Stell, Miels listened to them go on and on about what they'd like to do with him and Tristan. It all made him sick and Miels wanted nothing more than to leave, and was close to doing just that, when Betti finally muttered, "You seen the little thing recently?"

Stell tsked. "Passed her station yesterday. Closed. Such a lazy fucker."

The comment made Miels incredibly angry, but he ground his jaw down to keep calm.

Betti scoffed then the two were off to their own rooms giving Miels time to calm down before coming out of the crawl space and moving for his room in the King's wing.

8

ETEL

The fact that most of the servants in the palace hated her really didn't help Etel in situations where she needed the help to push out concoctions faster than normal. She was lucky to have one of the tailor's assistants, Atiana, come to her aid. That way she wouldn't have to deal with trying to get any servants within her suite. Most avoided it. Even those who didn't necessarily *hate* her.

The servants would be needed elsewhere anyway—preparing beds and rooms, and aiding the infirmary. Everyone's help would be needed to keep order in the palace while the select few aided with the victims of the explosion that had happened at the closest village.

Miels had gone to that village.

Gone to that explosion, even with the possibility of another going off.

She knew she should be more focused on getting out remedies and ailments quickly, but her mind continued racing to Miels. Kept racing to their kisses—the first one in his suite only a few days prior; the ones he'd given her every time he came to see her while she worked; the ones he gave to distract her and the one after finding out about her relationship with the other servants; the one he stole from her the night prior when he'd caught her coming back from her walk, pulled her into a corridor, and promptly chastised her for not being in her rooms when he went searching for her.

It'd been a whirlwind too good to believe, and now Etel could not imagine anything happening to Miels. Could not imagine losing his mischievous looks and annoying personality.

She and Atiana worked tirelessly for a few hours before they had enough vials to be sent to the infirmary—a feat the servants begrudgingly did every hour—and Atiana could take to her suite to rest.

Alone in her workstation, Etel could relax a bit as she crushed lavender and rosemary with her mortar and pestle. It allowed her the repetitive movement she required as her thoughts found their way back to Miels and her eyes watered as she pictured him getting hurt.

Then quickly berated herself for the negative thoughts she allowed.

She poured the lavender and rosemary mix into a larger mortar that already had the base for the serum that would be used to treat burns. They made plenty of the stuff already, but it was always good to have extra. Plus, it meant the hurt would have some to take along with them when they were ready to leave the infirmary.

"You're so beautiful deep in concentration like that, little creature."

Etel jumped, her mortar and pestle hitting the table as she turned to find Miels leaning against her table. She must've been deeply concentrated if she hadn't heard him come in—

though, he was a spy so maybe he was just good at being silent.

The breath left her as she took in his appearance and found nothing of worry. "You're okay?"

He didn't move, but watched her closely. "Completely."

She wanted to go to him. To crash into him and close her doors and live in a world where she was wrapped in his safe arms. She wanted to hold him, not in the hopes that he would never get hurt, but in case he ever got hurt. She wanted—needed—him to know she'd be there to hold him then too.

"Good," she breathed out instead.

His gaze narrowed on her as he pushed off the table and stood there. "I lied. Not completely."

Her eyes widened, chasing the air around him, looking for the source of his discomfort. "What is it?"

"You have yet to greet me."

That heart of hers jumped up her throat, then plummeted to the ground like the first night they'd met. She never initiated any of their moments in fears that he'd grown tired of her already.

But she was glad to hear quite the opposite from his lips.

Then she was running for him, uncaring in that moment if anyone were to pass by the open door of her workstation and see.

She crashed into his chest and wrapped her small stature around his much larger frame as his arms wrapped around her back so that she molded into him. This close, Etel could feel his heart beating, could breathe in his breath, could look into his beautiful eyes. "You're okay."

He nodded, but didn't allow her to drop her legs from around his waist as he held her. He leaned in and kissed her softly, almost like he was cherishing her taste. "Completely now."

S he hated that he'd had to run back to his Posse but understood the urgency. They had matters to take care of, she couldn't selfishly keep him to herself.

And honestly, she was glad too. Because they'd been lucky no one had passed the door and seen them. Etel couldn't imagine the rumors and hatred that would be thrown her way if the servants knew of...this, whatever it was.

Now, she was quite hungry, not having noticed her stomach in the hours she'd focused on the remedies and on Miels's safety. But now that all was calm, she needed the nourishment. Which also meant she'd need to brave whichever of the servants were in the kitchens.

Luckily, only Sona, a quieter servant than even Etel had been, was in the kitchen.

Etel gave her a nod of acknowledgment as she moved for a bowl to fill to the brim with the potato and lamb stew before covering it with a top to keep from spilling as she took it to her suite. She had no desire of eating down there tonight. Or any night, for that matter.

Etel placed the bowl on a tray as she readied a chunk of bread and a large bottle of water. She placed two small bell peppers, a small cucumber, and a tomato beside her bowl and was just about to leave when Betti and Jauc walked into the kitchen, Stell and Ini not far behind. Their faces instantly turned down at Etel's presence.

"Well, if it isn't our savior, the expert of remedies herself," Betti mocked.

Etel sighed. "I must return to my workstation."

Before Etel could pick up her tray, Stell grimaced at her. "Why don't you just suck their cocks, make yourself part of the Posse? Oh wait..."

Etel was struck, surprisingly not at the foulness of what she'd said but at the possibility. The fact that she had every intention to suck Miels's...penis when she had the chance. But the last thing she wanted was everyone thinking she'd grown her stations because of any relationship she had with him.

Jauc's lips twisted up. "Aw, you cannot speak to the child like that, Stell. Does she even know what a cock is?"

"She must." Stell stared at her straight, challenging her to argue. "With her embraces of the Master's whore brother, there's no way she wouldn't."

Etel swallowed but didn't know what to say. The only way Stell would think she were with Miels in any capacity was if they'd been seen.

"What're you on about, Stelly Belly?" Jauc's brows furrowed as he tried to keep a lightness to his mood.

"I just think it's funny that while we work our assess off, little remedy here gets to suck off a spy and get promoted. Is that why you needed your own chamber? He won't let you whore around in his suite?" Her eyes shined, like she was enjoying every second of putting Etel down.

"Stell, don't be ridiculous. *Miels* want that?" Betti ridiculed. "The man can have anyone at the palace. Plenty of us with finer looks and feels."

It would've made Etel laugh that Betti thought she had a chance with any of the Posse. She was old enough to be their grandparents, but the spark in her eyes told Etel she would do anything to rise in the palace. Maybe that's why they'd all so willingly believe Etel had done the same—they had no qualms about rising in that way, though she couldn't imagine Juac and Ini doing the same in their relationship. They were mean to her, but Etel wasn't blind to their love.

Etel knew she should say something. Stell obviously knew

something, and with her hatred, she would turn Etel's entire career into a fuck to the top.

"I saw them, Bet." Stell took an apple and slowly chewed off a bite before continuing. "While the rest of us were working, little expert here was wrapped in the spy's arms, kissing him. The door was wide open. I can only imagine now what happens when it is closed. I'd wondered why I'd heard talk of the spy heading to your workstation time and again lately. He becoming reckless with your whoring? No longer trying to hide his visits?"

Etel tried to keep her breathing calm. Because this couldn't be happening. She hadn't realized how much talk had broken out about her. Which was truly her first mistake. As a past servant, she should know better than the Posse how quickly gossip spreads.

Jauc, Betti, and Ini were all asking questions and throwing remarks, looking to her as if she were a whore when they all knew she hadn't done anything. Maybe they believed her a liar now too, faking her blushes to keep the secret of sleeping with the Master's brother a secret.

She didn't know how she expected this thing with Miels to roll out. But she knew that she'd been naive in thinking everyone wouldn't believe she'd fucked her way to the top. She knew that now.

And now that it was in her mind, she knew with certainty that nothing could happen with Miels. That they'd had their fun, but it would be over. She couldn't risk her career. It was all she had.

Etel swallowed back at the thought of not getting any more chances with Miels and picked up her tray, not caring what other jabs the others threw her way. "I must go. You lot have a nice night."

She'd been so stupid to run into his arms with the door open and to have truly believed no one had seen them.

In her suite, she sat at the table she made her remedies at and forced the stew down her throat. The realization of the end to this new thing she had with Miels had effectively wiped out her appetite, but she knew she needed the nourishment.

She had just about cleared her tray when the man all her thoughts revolved around walked into her room.

"It's been a long day, Etel." He moved to her so easily, reached for her face and leaned down to kiss her so comfortably.

As much as she wanted to return the gesture, she remained frozen and waited for him to pull back and look at her with furrowed brows. "This has to end, Miels."

"What?" He stood taller and looked down at her with a bit of panic in those perfect eyes.

"This." She gestured between them. "Whatever it is. It needs to end."

"Etel." He tried to cradle her face, but she pushed away.

"Let's be fair, Miels. You're starved for companionship. I'm an oddity to you, an innocence you can taint. You would've gotten bored at some point. Now, neither of us has to go through it. Neither of us will have to reap the consequences."

"Etel." He stepped up to her. "What the hell are you talking about?"

"You can run off with Tristan and find yourself a companion for your bed and easily forget about me, Miels. Go. Do it."

He tugged at her arms to bring her closer. "I don't wan—"

She pushed away and stumbled back. "Go, Miels. You have a month's worth of releases to make up for. Go!" She felt sick saying the words.

"Etel," he argued.

"I will not be the woman who slept her way to the Posse. I don't want it."

Understanding dawned in his eyes. "The others will talk whether we're together or not, Etel. They will still find something to say about you. They find many a things to say about us. It's inevitable."

She knew he was right, but still, she couldn't do this. This small career was all she had. He weathered the comments because the Posse was his family. But all Etel had was her career, she couldn't allow that to be sullied. "Go, Miels."

"Don't ruin this, Etel." He stepped forward, but stopped when she moved away from him. "Don't throw us away in fears of what the others, who already are jealous of your promoted position, will say of you."

"There is no us, Miels. We've kissed a few times. That's it."

"Etel," he begged.

"You'll forget about me as easily as you hadn't known of my existence, Miels. *Just find a few more women to be inside.*" Her stomach turned and she could feel her dinner race up at the thought, but she remained unmoving.

His jaw grit and he moved for the door. Before leaving, he turned to look at her over his shoulder. "You're the woman I want to be inside, little creature."

Etel hit the wall behind her and fell to a squat as he shut the door behind him. For the first time since meeting him, Etel allowed the tears to freely fall.

9

MIELS

When she had become his life source, Miels didn't know. But now he couldn't function properly. He needed her. Needed to touch her, to hold her, to kiss her. He needed her.

And she pushed him away. Rejected him.

Not because she didn't want him, that would hurt but it would be something Miels could accept. But she wanted him as deeply as he wanted her, he knew it. She wanted him yet hid behind the fear of the other's judgment.

After what he'd heard from them the night he'd met her, he couldn't entirely blame her. If they treated her so as innocent as she was, they'd rip her to shreds if they had any tidbit that signified she didn't deserve the things she had.

Miels hated them for it. Wanted to kill them for it.

But he also knew it was a new possessive side of him that thought those things. The other, more logical, side knew it would happen no matter what. Knew people spoke of him and Tristan as secreting themselves into Sparrow's life only so they could be part of the Posse. Knew they thought Miels was kept around because of Rosaelia's crush on him. There were so many rumors, Miels didn't bother remembering them all.

But Etel was new to it all. Up until a year ago, she'd been a quiet servant. She wasn't used to the talks of how undeserving their positions were. But Miels needed her to adjust.

Because he needed her.

And as he marched into the training fields, his cock reminded him that it too needed her. Hadn't stopped thinking about being inside her since the night they met. He needed that specific reminder to go away because while Sparrow was by Evony's side as she recovered from dispersing that powder, he would be leading training.

His sister had fallen and he had a constant worry for her, but do as he might, he still couldn't get Etel out of his mind. She was his constant. He needed her to need him.

He also needed her to know that she wasn't a servant anymore. Needed her to understand it. Though he respected their servants, Miels also knew the degrading way some could look upon any person who got to a position above them. Especially if they were at one point in the same station.

Etel had not yet accepted that as the Remedies Expert, she was now on the same level as any of the guards. Hell, she was on the same level as Ashtyn which basically made her just behind the Posse. Superior.

And if Miels was honest, with her skill, superior even to himself and Tristan.

But she wouldn't accept that. She was too ingrained in her past as a servant to know that she deserved her spot and deserved a spot within the Posse if he wanted her there.

She needed to get to the point where she understood that now that she was above the others' station, rumors would always spread about her. Not because he wanted to fuck her more than he wanted air, but because he needed her to *know* it. For herself.

"Ready positions," he barked out to the guards and watched as they stood straight and awaited his call. Knew they heard the edge to his tone.

Since the explosion, then the failed infiltration attempt with the poison that sent Evony to her bed, Miels was put in charge of trainings with James at his side while Tristan played damage control and Sparrow stayed by his woman's side. Truly, Miels did not envy either of their positions. Especially with the way he was feeling now.

He could make this a practice training session—Sparrow favored those making every one of their guards the best swordsmen—but that was the last thing Miels wanted at the moment. He'd incorporate it because of how useful and important it was, but he was normally the leader that made the guards burn.

"We'll be broken into threes. First group will condition, second will work suicides, third will throw the balls against the wall." The balls were each forty pounds which wasn't much for a couple of minutes, but each of these sections would last half an hour at least. "No breaks until time to switch. You'll have five minutes between. Then we spar."

James watched him with a worried furrow between his brows, but didn't argue his commands. It was something Miels truly respected about the man—that no matter how grueling a training, James was always ready to perform. To make it more difficult. He was the truest of warriors.

The guards, too, wouldn't argue his command, but Miels could see the worry on their features. He was normally the nicer of the trainers even when he was trying to make them burn.

Miels joined the conditioners, knowing leaving the balls

for the end, after suicides, would feel the worst, and he needed all the pain his body could bear at the moment. Anything to wipe Etel from his thoughts, if only for a few moments.

Conditions consisted of push-ups to rows to burpees, squat jumps, jumping planks, reverse lunges, pulsing supermans, and about a million crunches. Then a repeat of the entire thing until time ran out.

It all burned, but Miels still thought of Etel laughing, smiling, flushing. Imagined the taste of her lips and how desperately he wanted to taste the rest of her. Imagined lying in bed after he'd ravished her body and speaking all night. A feat he'd never wanted to do, but done in order to gain information. Now though, he wanted to keep her up all night and learn all those things about her that she continued to remind him he didn't know.

Was this how Sparrow felt with Evony's presence?

The beads of sweat rolled down his neck and made him imagine sweating as he fucked Etel for the umpteenth time. *Fuck.*

When time was called to switch groups, Miels walked over to the suicides field, passing James as he moved for the conditioning field.

"You okay?" James asked, the same suspicion in his eyes as before.

"Fine," Miels muttered and pushed forward, taking his gulp of water before getting into position for this round.

When time called to begin, Miels ran. Sprinted.

And for two glorious minutes, he ran to one end, then back and again with nothing in his mind. Clear. Free.

Then he caught eye of a servant, an innocent one he didn't particularly recognize, passing by the training fields, and all at once, he was bombarded with his desires for his little creature.

The sprints passed with the image of the little expert plaguing him.

And when time was called and he gulped down more water, he realized none of this was going to help him. Still, he moved for the ball wall, knowing this was all moot. He wouldn't get her out of his mind. She was his life force now, he needed her to survive. And if he couldn't have her, he'd be plagued with thoughts of her. Though to be fair, he'd been plagued with thoughts of her even while he had her. Much nicer thoughts though.

He knew the ball wall was the worst, and even still, it couldn't help him. His limbs burned with the work. His teeth grit so hard, he was sure they'd break out of his mouth entirely. And yet, not once did he break from throwing that ball. Not once did he take a mini break he knew everyone else had taken. Not once did he give himself the luxury. If Etel was pained with fearful thoughts of the rumors that would plague her, then he'd be pained with the physical exertion.

He had no delusions that his pain was the more difficult to bear.

When time was called for this final round and everyone began partnering up for the sparring finale, Miels saw everyone actively avoiding him. He didn't blame them.

James strolled up to him, sweat falling off of him in puddles. "Ready to talk about it?"

"It would make things easier, wouldn't it?" Miels smirked his way.

"So of course you won't do it." James rolled his eyes. "Don't worry. I was like that when I was falling for Gem too. Infuriated and in love and refusing to talk to anyone but her about it. Eve was so annoying around that time."

Miels froze in his spot and stared at his new friend. "Why compare our situations?"

James smirked now. "You are so obviously falling in love, my man."

Miels narrowed his gaze at the man. No he wasn't.

James shrugged. "At least to a man whose been through it." He shoved Miels's shoulder with his own. "C'mon, you don't have to tell me who it is. But fight me, let some of that frustration out."

The sparring did end up being the part of the entire training that helped Miels the most. Not because it got Etel out of his mind, but because he had an out for the frustration. Maybe he should've started with it after all.

As he walked to her suite, he thought back to the other thing James had said. That he was falling in love. That he was *obviously* falling in love.

It was impossible. Like Etel said, he didn't know her. And definitely not well enough to fall in love with her.

When he got to the suite, the sign telling others she was done for the day, apart from emergencies, hung. He considered knocking for a moment but opened the door instead.

He stepped in to find Etel at her table, picking herbs off of their stems.

She jumped at his presence and he loved the way her breath hitched as he shut the door behind him and left them alone together. "Miels."

He didn't move toward her, a feat he had to force his body to do. "I damn near tortured my men training today."

Those analyzing eyes took him in. "Oh?"

"I wanted to do something, anything, to get you out of my mind." He wanted to move for her but didn't do so. "It didn't work."

"Miels," she begged and he could see how much this distance pained her too.

"You want me, Etel, as much as I want you. You cannot deny that your body yearns for me as mine does for you. Cannot deny that you grow wet when you think of me."

Her eyes narrowed now. "You've quite the ego, Miels."

"And you've quite the way of making me hard as a rock, my little creature."

She sighed. "What are you doing here, Miels?"

"I won't forget about you, little one. And I won't be able to touch another woman." Ever, if he was being honest with himself. "I know you do not want *us*, but consider giving our bodies what they desire. We have a mutual problem that we can easily remedy."

"Miels," she said softly.

"I don't expect you to say yes," he interrupted. "At least not yet. But I needed you to know that I am at your disposal when you decide you need the release." He stood taller, bigger. "I am the only one at your disposal when you need the release, Etel." *You are mine.*

She swallowed. "Understood."

He stood then for long minutes and merely stared at her. When he finally got himself to speak again, the words fell out almost in a whimper. "I don't want to leave you."

Her eyes shut and she grabbed for the edge of the table for support. He could see the pain etched into every inch of her features. "I don't want you to either."

"But you'll still tell me to go." It wasn't a question because he knew the answer.

She slowly opened her eyes and met his gaze, then nodded.

"Etel," he grit out.

"Yes," she breathed out, barely audible, but still her words.

He stared at her another couple of minutes before he was

able to push his body to turn for the door and walk out into the corridor. Then lean into the wall to catch his breath and push aside the desire to turn back to her.

He moved for the King's wing, for the bath he needed before heading to his suite.

10

ETEL

It wasn't an entirely unreasonable proposition.

Both of their bodies yearned for one another and they would only be giving themselves the releases they needed. And she would be learning from him.

Plus, he had so many years of experience, she was sure to enjoy herself. She'd heard time and again from other women around the palace that a rendezvous had not gone particularly in their favor. That wouldn't happen with Miels.

Not only because he surely knew what he was doing, but also because she cried out for him every time she touched herself. Everything about him turned her on.

Etel was sitting in the herb garden by the kitchens, collecting ingredients to replenish her stock as she let herself breathe in the fresh spring air and clear her mind. Every so often, she saw one of the servants who still hated her walk past, but they thankfully paid her no mind. In times like these, Etel was glad to be invisible.

Even before she'd been made Remedies Expert, Etel had only been noticed by that group she used to spend her time with at the end of the night when everyone was settling and gossip could freely be spread. They would treat her like a child because she never had any gossip to add and blushed when they spoke of the especially spicy ones.

Even though they were all older than her, most of them were close enough to her age, and she knew they merely enjoyed being above her. It was one of the reasons Etel believed them especially infuriated with her promotion. Because they'd be angry about anyone getting promoted over them, but it especially vexed them that Etel had been that one.

Most of the other servants were envious, reasonably so, but they were never cruel to Etel. She wondered what they would say to her having any relations with Miels. Would they join the group of six—though really, it was dropping down to four since she hadn't heard from Alain and Brin in weeks— who already hated her? Would they look at her differently? Like she'd used her body to win a spot higher up in the palace. Would she be able to hold herself at all around the palace?

Etel breathed in the air as she gently took more lavender and placed it softly into her basket. Did she truly care so much about the others?

She hated that the answer was yes. Especially because she wasn't friends with anyone at the palace.

But did she want Miels with all her might? Also yes.

His offer gave her the chance to explore her sexual desires with the only man that had ever affected her so. It gave her the chance to have Miels for as long as he would take her before he got tired. And if Etel could continue being the wallflower who hardly got noticed, she could make sure no one found out, so her reputation was untainted and she could move on from the palace after Miels decided he was done with her.

But until then, she could enjoy herself. Enjoy all Miels

wanted to teach her and all she wanted to experience with him.

She stared out in the direction of the forests, knowing he was out with Tristan and Sparrow for their games of dagger throwing. She hoped the time with his brothers relaxed him. He'd always loved the dagger throwing time with the two men in the past when she would watch him from a distance.

Etel thoughtlessly placed more herbs into her basket as her gaze focused in on the forest as if she would be able to detect exactly where Miels was. She wanted to see him so badly. That grin he always wore with his brothers after coming home from throwing daggers was always so bright and big and always made Etel's body flush with want.

It was because of those lost thoughts that she didn't realize until she was basically standing in front of the herb gardens that the Princess's other cousin—the one that looked far more like her Southern roots—was before her.

Gemma.

She was beautiful with her deeper skin tone—though not as dark as her husband's—her hazel eyes, and those spirally russet curls. She, like Evony, also favorite trousers and a vest, and she moved like she was truly sure of herself.

Etel stuttered a moment when she realized the girl was looking at her. "Miss Gemma?"

A small smirk brightened Gemma's features. "No need for formalities. I simply saw you out here and wondered if you would like a hand?"

Etel's gaze dropped to what she was doing. She already had a basket full of basil, bayberry, and aloe vera. Each grouping separated with their own barriers, but they sat plentiful in the basket. Another basket was full of chamomile, rosemary, and dill. And this one with ginger, hibiscus, and now lavender. Etel still had more to pull and would spend a good amount of time individually carrying each basket up to her workstation. She'd been doing so alone for a year now, so the thought of help shocked her more than she cared to admit.

"Why?" She realized it may sound rude to ask, but she couldn't stop herself.

Gemma laughed as she grabbed for an empty basket and dropped to the ground. "I've always been curious about herbs and their remedies. I think it would be calming to do this with you. Plus, I think, when you are not busy, I'd like to learn more about these concoctions you make."

Etel didn't know what to say. Was she merely asking to learn about remedies or did she truly wish to be her friend?

Gemma's smirk said she knew her words shocked Etel, but the warmth in her eyes said she also understood that her peers were so hardly nice to her. She and James and Evony came to the palace from an unknown location. It made Etel wonder whether they had ever felt unwanted.

"What shall I begin picking then?" Gemma lifted her basket, solidifying that she would be working with Etel whether Etel liked it or not.

But Etel really liked it.

Especially because this was one of Miels's friends.

Etel smiled warmly. "You can begin with the lemongrass. In the other two compartments, you can add mint and thyme."

"Whatever you say, boss!"

As Gemma got to work, Etel couldn't help but watch her. As one of Miels's friends, it was nice to see the acceptance of Etel in her eyes. It made Etel wonder whether Gemma would accept her relationship with Miels, if she ever had one.

Etel looked back at the basket she almost had filled and knew with certainty that they may never have a loving relationship, and Gemma—or any of the Posse—may never find out, but they would have their lustful relationship.

Staring back out in the direction of the boys, Etel made up her mind. When Miels came back, she wasn't sure she'd be able to stay away from him, from that proposition he'd made her.

Reentering the palace from the herb garden put Etel back in the hallway that led directly to her past living quarters. She'd shared the space with the six she'd considered friends and they'd taken the spot closest to the herb garden for her. She'd thought them kind for doing so but part of her now knew it was only because they thought her childish and wanted to keep her happy as a child with this simple act.

Gemma had helped Etel move the baskets—seven in total —to her workstation before going off to meet with her husband. She was a lovely woman and Etel truly hoped she came to the workstation to learn some remedies. Etel would love to teach her. And something told her she'd be a much better student than Miels was.

Etel moved through the servant's corridor a final time with the seventh basket in hand as she tried to fight off the sadness being in this corridor brought her. She didn't miss their friendship, didn't want it back, but passing by her old quarters reminded Etel of the last group of people she had that cared for her. Knowing they never truly cared hurt deeper than it should.

Now, Etel only had Albert who cared for her. He lived in a close by village as an apothecary and was a brilliant old man. He always beamed at Etel's presence which only made Etel feel foolish now. Albert's reactions to her and those of the six she had thought friends were never the same. Albert was a true friend. The others were merely good enough acquaintances.

Etel resolved that she would need to go visit Albert some time soon. It was difficult given the rebellion for her to leave as the Remedies Expert, the only remedies maker at all, knowing her skills may be required on short notice.

But hopefully soon, this rebellion would be over and Etel could go to the old man and possibly teach *him* a thing or two. That last thought made her laugh to herself.

Etel was almost at her workstation when she tried to think farther back. Did she have friends before Albert, people who cared for her other than her parents?

She'd had friends growing up surely, and Etel could remember how kind they always were with her, but she'd enjoyed spending so much time with her parents that none of those friendships ever blossomed to anything strong enough. Now, she was glad for all the time she spent with her parents, glad to have those memories to cling to. Other than a few small possessions and painted frames, it was all Etel had of them.

And she cherished those memories more than any picture or trinket.

They'd loved her and it had taken almost everything out of Etel to lose them, especially at such a young age.

Maybe that's why she'd settled for the sort of friendship the six had offered—because she hadn't truly cared for a strong enough relationship. Albert's had only grown because he reminded Etel of what her father would've been like in even older age. No one else had broken that barrier that her parents and Albert had.

Until now.

Until Miels.

It was difficult to say he had broken any barriers because they weren't together and weren't even technically friends, but Etel knew she trusted him. She knew she cared for him in a way that she'd never cared for another, but that made him just as important to her life as her parents and Albert were. Etel wasn't entirely ready to think about what that necessarily meant, but she knew she cared for him.

And she believed—though that insecure, hateful part of her brain said she was wrong—that he cared for her too.

As Etel settled her final basket on her worktable and began putting all of the herbs away, she thought about Miels in all the times she'd watched him the three years she'd been at the palace—two as a servant, one as the Remedies Expert.

She remembered the first time she'd seen him. She'd known in that moment that she had never seen a more attractive male, even with Tristan as his likeness standing beside him. The two of them were with Sparrow, laughing and pushing each other around out in the greens as they moved from their private training room to the doors that led directly to the King's wing. They'd all been sweaty, muscles bulging from exertion, and exuding safety.

And so beautiful, Etel had been stuck in her spot as she'd been taking laps around the greens. She'd stared at Miels, dumbstruck that anyone could be so handsome, until he'd disappeared into the palace.

After that moment, she'd sought him out in the palace and hidden away to watch him. She'd been so confused as to why she was doing it, but she'd quickly figured that out when jealousy raged in her chest every time he and Tristan went out for 'fun' or to 'gather information.' She'd slowly been falling for the man, and it wasn't all based on looks either. She'd watched him so much, she knew things about him that others didn't; knew the way he cared for the Posse and the safety of his people; knew he had a huge heart to go along with that cocky, teasing ego.

It wasn't until she'd been moved from servant to Remedies Expert though that she'd truly been able to watch him closer.

As a servant, she worked most of her day and spent her free time working on remedies—it was how the Master Assassin had taken notice of her—so she only had slight moments where she'd glimpse Miels. In a way, those were simpler times.

When she became Remedies Expert, she spent most of the day working, but now remedies were work so her free time was used to do as she liked. Her brain and her heart always fought for what to do with that time, and normally that meant watching Miels. On the off chance her brain won out, she'd be walking the greens or the palace, or even on occasion, in the library.

But normally, Miels had been her obsession.

Talking to him this past week had only made that obsession grow. She knew now that it wasn't an infatuation with Miels, every time her heart raced as they spoke solidified that knowledge.

With the herbs put away and the baskets stacked off to the side, Etel sat at her table and leaned on a hand. She sighed, knowing exactly what she wanted to do about the Master Assassin's right-hand man.

11

ETEL

The seconds between knocking on the door and watching it open were short.

She knew it was stupid. That giving in like this would only lead to disaster. Because Etel knew herself. Knew once she had a taste of the Master Assassin's right-hand man, she wouldn't be able to stop.

But somehow she convinced that logical side of her brain that she would be able to stop. That there was no problem with seeking the release her body had yet to experience. And especially no problem in seeking it with the most handsome and desirable man she was sure to ever come by.

He was shirtless again, almost like he had a thing against shirts when he was in his suite.

"You came." He sounded genuinely shocked.

"Did you expect me not to?" Etel held herself high, afraid that any doubtful thoughts would send her running back to her suite.

"I expected you to fight your desires more. To torture me longer."

"I don't *want* to torture you, Miels." *I still can't believe you even want this.*

He stepped to the side so she was free to move in. "But you'll still refuse me."

"I'm here, am I not?" She stopped before his couch, the image of him lounging on it immediate in her mind, and turned to him.

"Because I offered you an out, the chance to get this without anyone finding out." He sounded pained as he closed the door and turned to her. "But if it is all I can get, then I will take it happily."

Guilt riddled up her throat. Especially at the reminder that the servants already had an inkling of something between them. Though she hadn't heard much talk of it. If Etel had to guess, it was because only Stell had caught them and it would already be difficult enough to convince everyone naive, bashful little Etel was with the whore Miels.

"I don't have much, Miels, I cannot lose my career."

"You wouldn't," he fought earnestly, taking a large step toward her. Then he shot out his hand to stop her protests. "No arguments. We're of two minds on the matter, but that's not why you're here."

No, it wasn't.

But she was far too nervous for the actual thing she was there for.

"If it is on your mind, then we can talk about it," Etel insisted.

He didn't respond as he studied her from head to toe. She was sure he could see her fidgeting in her spot.

"Are you nervous, little creature?" The pain from earlier was completely gone, replaced with unbridled desire.

Etel squared her shoulders. "No."

His chuckle was seductive too. Very much so. To the point where Etel had to clutch bits of her dress to keep still.

He stepped closer so they were only a few inches apart. "Do not lie to me, little one."

Though his tone was teasing, as Etel looked up into his eyes, she knew he was being serious. He wanted complete honesty from her.

And she had a desire to give him everything she could. Things that didn't threaten her livelihood, her future.

"I've never done this before," she breathed out.

He smirked, amusement shining in his eyes. "We've established that."

She swallowed. "And you've experienced plenty of it."

A hardness entered his eyes. "Trust me when I say, I've never experienced *this*."

"I just think it'll take some time...before I'm as comfortable being...as sexual as other women are." Etel stared at his chest as she spoke, unable even to look him in the eyes as she said it, spoke of being intimate. With him.

His index finger lifted her chin softly, the touch eliciting a small gasp mixed embarrassingly with a light moan. "I intend on spending the night between those legs, Etel. On kissing and licking every inch of your small frame."

Etel sputtered, trying desperately to hold herself still as she forced her gaze to not fall.

"If this is to happen, if I'm to spend the night between your legs as you spend the night between mine"—he said that last part with a twinkle in his eyes—"then I want you to look me in the eyes when you speak to me. Especially of these matters."

She swallowed, too nervous to say anything but knowing he needed to hear her. "Understood."

His thumb brushed her lips. "Good girl."

Her heart felt like it was ready to jump out of her chest as she stared up at him, anticipating the meeting of their lips.

And he knew it. Delighted in the way she fidgeted for his touch.

His lips brushed across hers as he said, "You're so enticing as you yearn for me, little creature."

Then his lips crashed onto hers and she finally allowed herself the freedom to touch him, feel the contours of muscle on display for her.

His hands merely cradled her face as he groaned into her mouth.

As she raked her nails down his back, he pulled back and stared into her eyes. "You're going to be honest with me?"

She nodded, mesmerized, then remembered to whisper, "Yes."

His smirk told her he was happy with her verbalization. "Have you ever touched yourself, Etel?"

Her cheeks burned so deep, she was sure this was the hottest they'd ever been.

On instinct, her gaze shot down to his chest.

She couldn't say a thing.

He chuckled, sexy and vindictive all at once, and pulled her face up by the chin again. "I'm waiting."

"Yes." The word was so inaudible, it was more a sound in the air than her admission.

His thumb brushed her bottom lip as he stared down at her. "What do you think of when you do so?"

She couldn't. They couldn't talk like this.

"If you'd like, I'll answer first." He was far too amused. "At least since the night I met you, I've been distracted with the need to come to the image of your beauty or the sound of your voice."

Etel couldn't breathe. This couldn't be happening. It was far too good.

"Miels," she whimpered low.

"Your turn."

She knew he wouldn't allow her to hide from the question, he'd pull her sexuality out and delight in it.

"You. I've..." Her gaze dipped to his chest in order to continue, but she forced herself to look back up. He was right, if they were to do this, she needed to be able to look at him, be honest with him. "I've always thought of you. Even before we officially met."

His eyes filled with black and Etel knew part of it was pride that she'd looked him in the eyes as she'd said that much. The other part was full desire, but that bit of pride made Etel happier than anything else.

He kissed her lightly, almost like a reward for her honesty, then pulled back to look at her again. "What do you think of?"

She cleared her throat. "Many things."

He laughed, low and delicious. "Give me one, my creature."

She blinked up at him for long seconds before blurting, "The most common, I imagine it's your hands instead of mine."

He grinned down at her, then stepped back. "Would you like me to undress you, or would you like to give me a show?"

Etel wanted both. Desperately wanted to feel his hands undress her, and at the same time, desperately wanted him to sit back and anticipate the feel of her skin as she teased him.

But she knew, could tell by the way he watched her, which one he wanted.

"Sit," she ordered, more authority in that small word than any she'd given before.

Again, pride shined in his eyes.

He moved past her to take his spot in the middle of the couch, legs spread wide, eyes never leaving her.

Etel was nervous, so much so she felt the jitters across her skin. But she forced them to go away, reminded herself constantly that the desire in his eyes was for her. Solely for her.

Those reminders helped immensely.

She wore a uncomplicated dress, so the mechanics of removing it were quite simple. Her fingers skimmed her body to her chest and reached for the strings holding the dress to her chest, his gaze hungrily following her hands.

She pulled on the strings and watched him stare at her chest rising and falling as the dress came loose at the top and she was free to pull the cloth apart until her breasts fell out.

Again, the fear of such an intimate act crashed into her, but it was all replaced by Miels's hips leaping off the couch like his cock was greedy for her. It felt powerful to have this hold over him.

She pushed the fabric until it pooled at her feet and she was standing before him as naked as the day she came to this world.

He licked his lips as his eyes roamed her flesh, and again, her skin prickled, but it was a high of excitement mixed with the embarrassment now.

"Now you sit," he order, his voice dark and guttural as he nodded to the end of the couch.

She didn't exactly know where he was going with this, but she didn't question him and did as he said.

When she was situated in the corner, facing him and waiting, yearning for the small inches of distance between them to be closed, he turned to her and lifted his hand. "How do you imagine my touch, Etel? Show me."

She knew her eyes widened at the demand, but she couldn't help it. A large part of her had thought he would take the lead where sexual matters were involved. She couldn't fathom being the one to lead.

"Show me, Etel. What do you imagine? Use me to send yourself to oblivion."

Her hand shook as she reached for his and brought it to her lips, needing to taste his skin a moment.

His fingers were calloused as any warrior's would be, and it made her wetter to feel it, to know the pure masculinity that went into creating hands like these.

"You're stunning, Etel."

She didn't think he was saying it to ease her. It looked as if he was mesmerized and couldn't keep the thought in. It drove her to continue with his request.

She dropped his hand, skimming those calloused fingers down her jaw to tease her throat before running down her chest and finally landing at her breasts. She circled one nipple then the other, and when she looked up to watch Miels, she met his gaze. She was surprised to find him watching her instead of his hand.

"How do you feel, Etel?"

She swallowed nervously and stopped his hand over her breasts, squeezing his fingers down over her nipple and involuntarily arching her back so her chest fell deeper into his touch. "Desirable."

He smirked and dropped his gaze to the way his fingers moved over her nipple. "You are desirable."

She didn't know where the confidence came from, but she reached for his other hand without being told to, moving it down her torso as she spread her legs before him.

He breathed deeply, her scent strong in the air, as his gaze dropped down to her center.

She brought his hand to her center and delighted herself in the way he hissed when his fingers touched her wetness. "Usually"—she moved his fingers to her opening, then back up without entering, her own breathing shallowing—"you tease me a bit before entering."

His gaze shot to hers when she spoke, lust so strong it was ready to shred the world apart and put it back together in his eyes.

She licked her lips and realized the moment his gaze dropped to her lips that it'd be seductive. "Usually"—she moved his hand to her other nipple, letting his fingers peak at their will as she moved his other hand up and down her cunt, stopping to play at the clit a few times—"when my fingers enter me..."

He groaned, his hips thrusting lightly into the air as he faced her.

"I imagine it's your...cock..."

"Etel," he growled.

"But sometimes, I let the image stay as your fingers. Let the thought of your hand hitting me every time your fingers play with me send me to...oblivion."

She lowered his hand until his palm pressed into her clit and the tips of his two fingers stopped at her center. He spread them so only his middle slipped into her slowly, allowing her to adjust to having him touch her.

She moaned and arched again, allowing his hand over her breasts to do as it pleased as she held on to his forearm. But the other hand, she led, slowly moving it in and out of her and moaning as his palm teased her clit perfectly.

The next time his fingers pulled out, he added a second as he filled her.

She moaned, though it wasn't loud by any means. Her Northern roots paralyzed her from making any noise at all a moment before she pushed them aside. She wouldn't let customs and ideals ruin this moment.

As his palm hit her and his fingers filled her, and his other hand played with her nipples, Etel completely let go of control, her head falling back to enjoy the moment. She reached up for Miels's neck and pulled him close, needing to taste him as she got closer to that oblivion.

His tongue clashed with hers and sent her over the edge immediately.

He didn't stop kissing her as she rode his fingers through her climax. He didn't stop kissing her as she came down from her high, cunt clutching the ends of her orgasm around the fingers still pumping into her.

When finally he broke away, he looked down at her, proud. "That's my girl. My perfect, little creature."

She beamed up at his praises, loving that he was as pleased with what they'd just done as she was.

She whimpered, missing the touch, as he pulled his fingers out of her. His other hand held her jaw still as he kissed her again.

When he pulled away, he brought the fingers that had just been inside her to his mouth and sucked, lapped at the palm that had been pressed into her. "Mm, my Remedies Expert, make me a tea filled with your taste, and I'll happily drink it to my death."

12

MIELS

She would be the death of him. He was ready to suffocate in this moment. In her.

Miels moved slowly, pushing himself off of Etel to stand before her, his erection straining against his trousers.

She still breathed hard, her legs open as if inviting him to slip in.

Miels pulled on the ties to his trousers, mesmerized with Etel as she watched him as the fabric slipped down his muscled thighs. Her breath caught, and he knew it was partly for the fascination of seeing a cock for the first time in her life, though he allowed his ego to believe it was entirely for the size of his manhood.

He stepped out of the pants and stopped before her. "Do you want to touch it?"

She nodded, mesmerized, before remembering herself and whispering, "Yes."

Though she whispered it, Miels could hear the difference in this sound compared to the words of before. This one wasn't whispered out of bashfulness or mortification, but by the simple fact that she was too hypnotized otherwise. It made Miels feel more wanted than any long list of women he'd whored with before.

Her fingers didn't wait for him before slipping up his thighs, her nails eliciting a moan from his lips as they moved through his thigh hairs to the base of him. She stroked him with fascination before her thumb played with the tip, spreading the bit of liquid around.

"You're quite large." She didn't meet his gaze as she watched her thumb play and it was one instance where Miels could forgive her the act. "Are all men this large?"

"No." Miels didn't say it to brag, he simply knew he was gifted larger than most men.

She looked up at him through her lashes, and the innocence of it made his balls tighten. "Will you take me now?"

He cradled her jaw and watched, mesmerized as his thumb played with her bottom lip before saying, "No." He delighted in her displeasure before moving away from her and taking his seat in the middle of the couch again. "You will take me."

"Miels," she gasped, no longer as confident as before.

This was exactly why he wanted it done this way.

"Etel," he said softly, allowing her the time to process.

She breathed deeply before meeting his gaze and crawling to his side. "I trust you," she whispered against his lips before kissing him.

Miels hadn't expected such small words to have such a large effect, but his heart pumped with deep, unbridled pleasure.

When he pulled out of the kiss, he held her face between his hands. "It will hurt, Etel. Even more so because of my size."

She nodded and repeated, "I trust you."

His lips quirked into a small smile as he led her thigh over his to straddle him, her wet cunt sliding down his length and making them both moan out in pleasure.

She sat up, but because of her small stature and his much larger one, it didn't allow for much space for them to watch him slide in. He gripped the base of his length and paid attention to Etel's reactions as he played with her slit.

"Dig your nails into me if you need to, little creature. Make me bleed as I will make you." He quite liked the picture it brought up.

She nodded, her gaze never leaving his as she waited, and finally, he stopped his tip at her entrance and slowly moved her down. He allowed her to control the pace, stopping to allow her body to adjust to his size as needed and feeling the sting of her nails bite into his shoulders. Through it all, he was mesmerized by her beauty, not to mention the orgasm wrenching pleasure being inside her cunt brought on. He'd never had to fight the release so early on.

She settled at his base, then moved again to empty herself before sliding down his cock again. When she was more comfortable with his intrusion and didn't need to pierce into his skin so deeply, she murmured against his lips, "Take your pleasure."

His haze disappeared. "What?"

"Take your pleasure," she repeated. "I know the woman is hard to finish on her first time. It is why you pleased me first. Now, take your pleasure."

He didn't let her move on his length, holding her still around the waist as his hand held her face in place. "Believe me, Etel, it is not why we focused on your release first. I intend on doing a lot more of that, though my tongue may want the turn my fingers got next." He took pleasure in her flush. "And trust you me, you will come now and every time we are together. I will not allow myself the release until you find yours."

"But you don't have..."

His thumb stopped her. "I do. I need your release as much as you do."

She nodded, then pushed off of him before sinking back down slowly. Holding off would be far more difficult than he imagined.

While one hand helped her keep pace, the other slipped to her clit, rubbing it as she moved. Her eyes fluttered as she let out a moan.

None of her moans were loud, but they were all exciting in a way Miels hadn't known possible. He'd always imagined loud as the best way to be, but hearing Etel, he knew nothing was better than this. These intimate sounds made only for his ears.

Though he imagined in time, he could make her scream loud enough for the whole of the King's wing to hear.

She watched him with a small smile as she moved atop his cock, her hands moving from his shoulders to feather around his neck. She leaned down to kiss the spot her fingers touched. "I don't like these bruises."

A light chuckle escaped him as he controlled his breathing. "I deserved them."

"Oh, I'm sure you did." She kissed the bruise again before looking him in the eyes. "I just don't like seeing you hurt."

His fingers pinched her clit before rubbing circles again, watching her pleasure grow as she took him. "I need you to come, baby. Because hearing those words from you make it impossible for me to hold back much longer."

She leaned into him, her whimpers answer enough before she managed, "Trust m..." Her moan rang in his ears and nearly made him spill entirely. "I'm...about..."

She couldn't warn him as her pleasure hit and she gave him the loudest of her moans yet, her cunt clenching around his cock and forcing him to pull out of her immediately. Unfortunate, given how desperately he wanted to feel her clench around him.

But he knew his body and was just able to pull from her as he came, spilling his seed between their bellies.

When they came back from their highs, she looked between them at the mess he'd made. "Why'd you do that?"

The thought of her falling pregnant both scared him and brought joy to his heart. "You did say you didn't want others knowing, did you not, little creature? If you were to fall pregnant, they'd surely speak."

She rolled her eyes and watched him with amusement. "I'm the Remedies Expert, Miels."

"I'm aware, love." He pushed her hair back to memorize every bit of her beauty.

She, too, played with his hair. "I'm the Remedies Expert. I make concoctions to stop pregnancies for the other women in the palace all the time, Miels."

He watched her intently. "How effective is it?"

"As much as your pulling out." She kissed the bridge of his nose. "There's always still a chance, but much lighter."

He grinned. "Next time I won't pull out."

She looked just as pleased as he felt with the statement.

13

MIELS

They were in the forests so early in the morning, the servants wouldn't have a chance at having caught them going in. And when they returned—separately even though it was the last thing Miels wanted—Etel could use the excuse she was looking for something specific for her remedies.

But he wanted to enjoy some time with her out of either of their suites. He loved the outdoors and wanted to cherish it with her. If they couldn't be out in the greens of the palace, coming into the forests was Miels's next best option. And they weren't so far out, so it would still be completely safe. He would never put Etel in any danger, no matter how much he wanted to spend time with her outside of their suites.

It had rained in the night and now the leaves and grass underfoot were wet, but with the rising sun, the mud wasn't as much as it could be.

He had brought the daggers he normally used when out dagger throwing with Tristan and Sparrow, and intended on teaching his little expert how to hold one.

Then maybe how to throw one.

Etel shrugged as she watched him pick out which dagger to start with. "I taught you some remedies. It only makes sense that you would teach me your expertise."

Miels smirked back at her. "I've already given you a glimpse at my expertise. And when we get back to my suite, I intend on showing you more."

Etel blushed, but she looked almost...annoyed? "Please do not remind me of *all* the other women you've been with."

Miels's smirk dropped, and he turned immediately for her. He liked her jealous, but he didn't want to hurt her. He couldn't even imagine her with another man. The fact that she had to deal with all of the women of his past felt too fucked up. "Etel, I didn't mean..."

She held up her hand to stop him. "I know." She stood taller and stuck out her hand, grabby fingers ready. "Now gimme the dagger."

He grinned because she was cute like this. He handed the dagger over slowly. "Be careful, Etel. This isn't one of your herbs. You could truly be hurt."

She rolled her eyes. The annoyance filled with amusement now. "Yes, Mr. Big Bad Spy. Now"—she held it and let the finger of her opposite hand slide over the blade—"how do I throw this thing and land it in a tree?"

Miels laughed. "Aren't we getting ahead? You've only just held the thing. Don't you think you need more instruction on how to handle yourself with it first?"

She smirked, raising the blade to point at him, and allowed her glowing eyes to stun him. "Are you afraid your girl is gonna be better than you on her first try?"

Miels's eyes shined, and his smile was large as he stepped closer to her, the tip of the blade pressed to his shirt. "You're my girl?"

She most definitely was, but given how much she refused their relationship, he was shocked to hear it off her tongue.

She froze, and it was obvious she hadn't meant to say those words. Or even noticed they'd slipped out until he said anything. "No...I...uh...I meant..."

Miels laughed as he softly knocked the hand with the blade to the side and stepped closer to her, taking her face in his hands. "You're my girl, Etel."

"Miels..."

He kissed her slowly, then looked into her eyes. "You're." He kissed her chin. "My." He kissed the tip of her nose. "Girl." He kissed her forehead, lingering there to force his heart to calm down. He needed to take things slower with her than he'd like to.

When he leaned back enough to look into her beautiful brown eyes, there was hope there, but it was obvious she wasn't going to verbalize it. Instead, she rolled her eyes again and pushed him away. "You're supposed to be teaching me."

Miels bit into his lower lip, his cock hardening more as he watched her. "Be careful, little creature. Roll your eyes at me again, and I may have to teach you a lesson or two about respect."

She quirked her brow, indignantly as she watched him. "What, exactly, will you teach me?"

He stepped behind her and collared her throat before she could turn to him. His other hand slipped to her ass and squeezed. "I think this little bit of dessert needs a reddening, my creature. Maybe that'll fix your attitude."

She flushed, obviously understanding how badly Miels now wanted to spank her, but said nothing of it. Eventually, she breathed out, "Teach me the dagger, Miels. Soon we'll have to be back to the palace, and I want to learn a bit before we head in."

Miels wanted to push for some more, but she was new to the whole sexual arena, so he would take it slow. He moved around her again and grabbed for a dagger of his own.

He stood beside her and looked down at her with as much seriousness as he could muster with all the amusement he was feeling watching how determined she was. "Well, little creature, if you'd like to throw the dagger, then this is what it should look like."

Miels let the dagger fly from his hand and watched Etel's reaction as it soared through the air. He didn't need to follow it to know it had stuck into the trunk of the tree. Etel's awed reaction was far better in any case.

"Now your turn." He smirked down at her.

She narrowed her eyes on him, but didn't back down. Instead, she turned the tables, the little minx. "Why don't you come behind me and show me how it's done, Miels?"

The little seductress of a creature.

He wrapped his arms around her waist before one skimmed down her arm to the hand holding the dagger. "Anything for you, my creature."

Word had come back regarding the plague and none of it was of much help. From what each of the four missives said, it was a normal sickness and most seemed to be making full recoveries. That last bit at least eased some of Miels's worry, and made him wonder if, in actuality, the sorcerers of the Island Nation truly hadn't gone after the Northerners. So close to the Island Nation and the colder climate, it wouldn't be shocking for the northernmost part of the lands to have a sickness running through it.

James finished reading the final letter as he, Tristan, and

Miels sat around the round table at the top room of the palace. The one Sparrow and Evony had used a few weeks prior for their own personal fun.

Right where James sat now, though Miels wouldn't tell him that. He liked to tease the lot, but Evony truly was James's sister, so he'd give the man that reprieve.

Tristan shrugged. "Hopefully that means we can set it aside as a concern for right now. Keep the men posting, but nothing to worry about yet."

James smirked and leaned back in his chair, his hands clasping behind his head. "Yes. We do have a wedding to prepare for. It is nice to have one less thing to worry about right now."

Miels smiled unconsciously. He still couldn't believe his brother—the literal Master Assassin and Broody Magnificent —was getting married. He remembered that smile that ate up Sparrow's face when he and Tristan were in his suite to congratulate him and laughed; remembered Evony's presence on the table and laughed some more.

"Yes." Miels faced the Southerner. "You ready to give little Evie away?"

James rolled his eyes. "She has that man by the balls. The very least of my concerns is how much he loves her."

"Is that why Eve let you marry Gemma? Gem have you by the balls too?" Tristan asked with amusement.

James winked. "In more ways than one, mate."

"Where is little Gem this fine day?" Miels leaned back in his own chair, enjoying the moment of peace with his brothers.

"In the herb garden. She saw the Remedies Expert there the other day and said she's gonna start lessons to make concoctions and remedies. She's so excited, she's out learning more of the herbs."

Miels froze in his seat, then forced himself to calm, glad

neither of the men were paying attention to him. Gemma had been with Etel in the herb garden. They'd spent time together.

And were planning on doing so again.

Often if what James said was true and Gemma would be taking lessons.

Miels knew Etel hadn't mentioned it because she was afraid to make more of the situation than it was and end up being disappointed so he wouldn't speak on it, but it made him happy. At least in a situation like this, Etel might see that she is truly on the same level as him where superiority stood.

Etel was a great teacher too, from every single one of his earlier lessons with her, so he knew Gemma would have a great time. His lips tipped up at the thought of the two of them at that worktable, slicing and crushing and mixing ingredients. He imagined himself and James coming to them after a grueling training session for a kiss before heading out to wash up. He imagined trying to convince them to join, which he didn't see being all too much of a problem.

"What's got you smiling like that?" Tristan interrupted his thoughts.

Miels forced the images out of his mind, knowing he'd bring them back up at a later time, and caught his brother's gaze. "Just wondering what fun we can have pissing Spar off once they're married. Eve is definitely gonna be on our side."

Tristan chuckled as James said, "Oh, for sure. She's gonna love pissing Sparrow off. It'll lead to angry sex, and she's gonna *love* angry sex."

They all laughed at that. If they were sure of one thing, it was that Evony would tease the ever-loving shit out of Mr. Grumps, then enjoy every moment of it when he taught her a lesson.

Maybe it wasn't such a bad thing Edmund didn't necessarily see her as a daughter. He probably wouldn't want to know all that about his daughter, and they all knew the types of things Evony would like to do—and definitely will end up doing—to the Assassin.

"Don't we all," Tristan murmured as he let his head rest on the back of his seat, eyes closing. He was likely imagining angry sex and the fun he's had with it.

James's head leaned back too, and he also closed his eyes. There was no doubt—especially with that smirk on his face—that he was thinking about all the times he and Gemma had fought and the fun they'd had because of it.

As Miels rested his head back and closed his eyes, he realized he needed to make Etel angry at some point. Just to show her how great angry sex was.

14

ETEL

There was a nook in a corner of the palace, up on the third floor, that was unbeknownst to most.

It was Etel's most favorite of spots.

Well, it had been. Now, Miels's bed was her most favored.

It was not only a quiet nook, but it also gave Etel a clear view of the greens below and a perfect line of sight to the chapel that the Master Assassin and the Master Magician would be using.

She still couldn't believe Miels had trusted in her enough to tell her who Evony truly was—the Princess's twin and thus an heir to the Northern Lands, *and* the Master Magician.

He'd said he trusted her to keep it secret as the Posse had been and that she needed to know if she were to attend the wedding with him. She'd make sure his confidence in her wasn't wasted and would keep the secret to her death.

But she wouldn't be attending the wedding.

He'd been upset at her refusal, but it was a small occasion held only for Sparrow and Evony's closest companions. She hadn't wanted to intrude.

And Miels had been understanding. At least for the fact that it was a moment for the two Masters' closest family.

Not to mention, she and Miels had only been together in secret thus far. Etel couldn't risk her relationship with a Posse member coming out. Because this lovely part of her life where she got to share her body with Miels would come to an end, and she needed to be prepared to continue on with her profession. She wouldn't be able to do that if all believed she'd slept her way to the top.

It pained her too much to comprehend when she thought of her time with Miels ending. So instead, she watched from her window as the King's Posse gathered into the chapel, and a few minutes later, emerged in enthusiastic glory.

They all laughed together excitedly before Sparrow had Evony's hand in his and they were off to the little cottage at the edge of the palace property for some semblance of a honeymoon.

Then the others were coming together and laughing so hard, Etel could only imagine the types of jokes they were making of their friends. The types of jokes coming from Miels's mouth. His dirty, beautiful mouth.

She still couldn't believe she'd kissed that mouth. Couldn't believe that mouth had been on her, not once but every night since she'd gone to his room that first time. He'd tasted every single inch of her, and she'd returned the favor, a fact she remembered in every alone moment she had. She could still taste him on her tongue from that morning as she looked out the window to the happy group.

It was all so entirely unbelievable, she spent every day scared it would be the one to end it all. It was frightening to imagine going back to a life where she slept in her own bed, on her own, without the touch of her handsome spy.

It was even worse to imagine said spy in the arms of

another woman if he went back to whoring. Or in the arms of another woman he'd inevitably fall in love with.

Etel was strong in many ways, but she could not imagine herself strong enough for that. Though she would try.

And fail.

Because it would be torture.

So she would leave the palace for work elsewhere. And if she continued to keep her reputation clean, she'd have no problem finding said work. Or maybe she'd go back to Albert?

Miels, Tristan, and James pushed each other around the greens as they all headed back for the palace. She knew they would be headed for the dining hall for a celebratory dinner even though husband and wife would not be joining them. The Posse would celebrate for the married couple as said married couple celebrated with one another. It made Etel smile—the love they all had for one another.

Etel wanted to celebrate with Miels, steal him away from the group and have him take her in one of the small rooms in a corridor by the dining hall. In one of those rooms that were hardly used.

Her moans weren't too loud, and if she tried, she could keep herself from making too much noise at all. And he could do the same.

As Etel watched them disappear into the palace, she pictured it—Miels's strong body pressed into hers as her back collided into the wall. The feel of his large hands easily lifting her and his too-big-to-be-allowed cock sliding in and out of her.

She made herself wet instantly with the thought.

Which was ultimately the deciding factor. She would wait for them to finish their dinner, then hopefully catch Miels on his own.

She moved to the corridor with all the unused rooms and

found a spot in a darkened corner she could settle. The ground was quite comfortable as she sat back against the wall, the excuse that she was merely lounging ready lest anyone pass by and ask what she was doing on the floor.

Now, she had to wait.

And though they sat in the dining hall for over an hour, the muffled chorus of laughter passing through the large doors, Etel didn't feel the time. She spent much of it thinking of Miels as he trained and the precision he put into his movements.

When, at last, the doors opened, Miels was not alone.

He was accompanied by James and Gemma, but Etel had a feeling getting him away from the married couple wouldn't be difficult.

She scurried off the ground and caught Miels's arm as he was passing the dark corner she was situated in.

He froze and she could tell he was about to use his strength to attack when his gaze landed on her and his lips widened as he called out to the others, "You two have fun."

He pushed Etel into the darkened corridor without waiting for a response—which never came—and his wide smile touched Etel's. "You plan on surprising me like this often, my little creature? I quite enjoy it."

She shook her head as she walked backward, leading them to the room at the far end. "I was watching the wedding, and seeing you so happy brought this picture up in my head." She pushed the door open without turning away from him and shoved them inside. "I made myself so wet just thinking about it. You won't have to get me ready. You know how badly I wanted to rip you out of the dining hall while I waited?"

He pushed her into the far wall.

He didn't have to ask what she'd imagined, he knew she liked walls.

"You should've done it, love. I would've had absolutely no

problem with that." He hefted her into his arms. "In fact, it would've been quite the way to wrap the evening." He kissed behind her ear. "Though, I must say, this is pretty amazing too."

She giggled as she pulled on his hair and brought his lips to meet hers.

~

Unfortunately, their tryst in that room wasn't the end of the evening. Etel needed to go back to her suite to make sure there weren't any emergency remedies required—which was rare—and to clean up. Then she'd make her way back to Miels's room for the night.

Remembering the way he grumbled when she told him to go on without her and she'd meet him at his suite still brought a smile to Etel's lips. He was such a cute little baby sometimes.

That smile faltered when she caught Gemma leaning against the wall to her suite, waiting.

"Did you need something?" Etel asked, worried that an emergency concoction would actually be of need.

Gemma smiled warmly. "A nausea shot please. It just randomly hit. I think my stomach wasn't a fan of something I had at dinner earlier."

Etel moved into her workstation and toward the shelf that held any extra vials she made in low times. She reached for one of the nausea vials she had prepared, knowing Gemma's stomach couldn't wait at the moment.

She handed it to the girl, then watched her closely as she smiled and took the shot in one go.

Gemma set the vial down on the workstation and met Etel's brown orbs again. "Thank you. Maybe I can stop by in the next few days? Begin learning anything you'd like to teach me."

Etel's brows shot up. "You were serious about that?"

Gemma laughed. "Of course. Call me an apprentice."

Knowing she wasn't truly the Princess's cousin didn't mean Etel found it any less odd to think of her as a station lower, which she would be if she were Etel's apprentice.

It was like she could read the indecision in her eyes because Gemma added, "I think we're of the same status, Etel. But if it will make you uncomfortable calling me an apprentice, then I shall be a peer, a companion whom you teach a few concoctions to."

Etel's brows narrowed. "Are you sure this is where you want to be? You're plenty good at reading minds. Maybe you should be down in interrogations."

Gemma laughed. "I'm no good with reading minds, Etel. I'm good with reading how my friends are feeling."

"We're friends?"

"I'd hope we could be."

"Why?"

Gemma watched her a moment, probably reading more into her than Etel cared to show, then answered, "We know what it's like not to fit in, not to be wanted. We know what it's like to feel like you don't belong anywhere, and right now, you feel like you don't belong in your station. Maybe while you help me with these remedies, I can help you see you're wrong."

Etel's smile was close-lipped and small, but it was genuine. "I don't know if I want your friendship if you're going to read me like a book every second."

Gemma's laugh was large and bright this time. "You'll get used to it, babes. Eve and James certainly are."

Etel laughed with her as she nodded, clearing off her work-station and reaching for two more nausea vials to hand over.

She glanced down Gemma's form before meeting her eyes again. "For the next couple of days. It'll be the first thing I teach you when you begin."

Gemma's eyes shined like they were sharing a secret—which they probably were—as she took the vials. "Thank you, friend."

"You're welcome, friend."

Alone in her suite, Etel tidied up the last of her station before grabbing a change of clothes and heading out. The sign on the wall said closed unless of emergency, so people didn't know she wasn't actually in her suite, and every night, she hoped there wasn't an emergency that showed she was truly not there.

On her walk along the darkened walls in order to keep hidden, Etel thought back to her interactions with Gemma thus far. The girl was sweet and genuine and someone Etel could truly see herself becoming friends with.

That now put Atiana and Gemma as potential friends.

It felt nice. Going from zero friends and a life of loneliness to possibly two friends and the man she was falling for.

She didn't think too much about any of it in order to keep her hopes at bay, but she couldn't contain the smile at the thought. She wouldn't be so lonely any longer.

15

ETEL

Miels was playing a very dangerous game.

But Etel couldn't lie she enjoyed it.

He knew to be extra careful not to be seen coming to her suite now. The door to her suite was open for anyone to come in, yet Miels had scurried beneath her work-table anyway. She'd been shocked to see the cloth he'd dropped over the table and had hardly asked what it was for before he'd told her to continue working and gotten beneath it.

Not a moment later, his hands had trailed up her legs beneath her skirts, then his breath had hit her skin.

Now, Etel tried to remain unresponsive to his teasing as she ground ginger and rutabaga in a mortar.

His hands were caressing her legs, up the sides of her calves and thighs and back down the back of her thighs and calves. All the while, he laid soft kisses on her thighs, her hip bones, the apex of her thighs.

It all made Etel wiggle in her spot, but she didn't stop or rush him. She liked this teasing Miels.

Until she was no longer alone, that is.

King Edmund turned the corner and entered her suite and mortification traveled through Etel's body. He didn't know that one of his spies was currently beneath the table, but Etel felt like he could tell.

"Remedies Expert!" He smiled at her, and she felt Miels stiffen beneath her skirts. "I'm glad to have caught you. Are you too busy?"

"N-No," she stuttered. "Just stocking up, Your Highness." And as an afterthought, "Oh, and Etel would be fine, sir."

The King was too handsome of a man and his smile was warm as he watched her. "I'm glad to have caught you. I was wondering if I could ask you a favor, Etel?"

His handsomeness plus his sexy voice when he said her name shouldn't be allowed.

Etel wanted to give a hundred percent of her attention to the King, but Miels's lips on her skin again, his hands continuing their caresses, caught most of her attention.

She tried to kick him away without being obvious, but that only made him shove her legs wider before his tongue slipped through her folds.

Etel swallowed back and cleared her throat, fighting off the gasp that wanted to let out from the feeling of his mouth on her. Instead, she met the King's gaze as unaffected as she could muster. "Anything, Your Highness."

By the look he gave her, she wasn't all that convincing. "I am healthy as can be, but I like to keep sure. I was wondering if you could make me some gut concoctions. I'd like to keep the responsibility of running a land off my daughter for as long as possible."

Etel wanted to smile at the warmth that was obvious when Edmund spoke of Rosaelia, but she gasped instead as two fingers shoved inside her without warning, the heat in her belly rising as Etel gripped her worktable and tried to hide her reaction from the King.

He noticed anyway.

"Are you all right, Etel?" He stepped up, but stopped when Etel threw up a hand to stay him.

She bit her lip to fight the whimpered gasp Miels's suck on her clit was trying to force out of her, then answered, "Just stubbed my foot, Your Highness."

"Ah, yes," the King smiled. "Those do hurt more than they should. And please, Edmund is all right, especially if I am to continue seeing you."

Etel bit into her lower lip and dropped her gaze to the table as she nodded to the King. She couldn't meet his eyes from embarrassment, and she knew she was about a second away from coming from Miels's mouth and fingers. She was glad the rain that could be heard through the cracked window was hiding the wet sounds of her cunt.

When a gasp fought its way out, Etel's cheeks blazed in more embarrassment for what was happening before the King, but also in fury. Because Miels's mouth and fingers had left her, softly kissing and trailing her legs instead. The ass was playing with her.

Edmund took another step closer to the table, thankfully on the other side. "Are you sure you're all right, Etel?"

Etel finally forced herself to meet his gaze. "Fine...Edmund. I just...tried to step on the foot I jammed, and it hurt more than I was prepared for."

She wasn't sure if he believed her since she wasn't the best of liars, but he didn't push her for more. Instead, he said, "Hopefully no more pain befalls you then. How about I leave you to make the drinks I need?"

"Of course."

"No rush, Etel. Make them when you have time. I am not in such dire need of the remedies."

A small smile lifted her lips as she said, "Okay, Your Highness."

Edmund's eyes twinkled with a teasing glint like he would reprimand her for being so formal again at the same moment Miels kissed her clit and she had to grind her teeth together to keep her composure.

Thankfully, Edmund didn't say much more, seeing the teasing nature of Etel's words, and left her be.

When he was gone, and Etel was sure she heard no one else in the halls, her hand gripped Miels's hair through her skirts. "I'm going to kill yooooo..."

He sucked on her clit and shoved those two fingers back inside her as he chuckled, the vibrations like heaven against her sensitive nub. She could feel her arousal slipping down her thighs as he continued on. No doubt the evidence of her arousal was coating every inch of his stubbled jaw. The thought made her hornier.

Miels pulled his mouth away, fingers still moving, as he demanded, "Keep working, little creature."

Etel didn't want to, but she knew his mouth wouldn't continue lest she did so, so she picked up a new mortar and pestle to grind other ingredients together. She needed to cut some bark and more ginger, but she didn't trust herself with a knife at the moment.

Then Miels continued, his mouth licking her folds before sucking at her clit as those fingers worked her. It was torture to try and concentrate on her work, but she knew it was the only way to get him to continue. And it almost made it more intense —not allowing herself to relax into this overwhelming feeling.

Just as she was on the precipice of the most intense orgasm

of her life, the Master Assassin walked through the doors with a small smile and a polite, "Good afternoon, Etel."

Miels pulled his mouth and fingers away instantly, moving back to teasing her legs with soft touches. Her arousal soaked down her legs with the removal of his fingers and made her wiggle for comfort. She wanted *his* arousal sliding down her legs.

More so, Etel wanted to throw the entire table across the room in frustration, but remained poised in the presence of the Assassin, knowing her body was flushed from Miels's attention and knowing there was nothing she could do about that. "Master?"

He eyed her curiously, probably trying to analyze what was happening, before that polite smile came back. "I was wondering, if you weren't too busy, if you could begin on remedies for the guards. Each one will need a set of two pain, two headache, and two nausea vials. Anything else, they will come to you personally, but I need them to have those."

Etel's eyes widened slightly. That was a lot of vials. There were hundreds of guards. "Of course, Master. That's what I'm here for!"

It was a lot, but she enjoyed these tasks. They kept her busy in a way making extra vials didn't.

Miel's tongue swiped up the inside of her leg and Etel's entire body froze, both loving his tongue on her and knowing the Master Assassin was the best at reading people. The very last thing she wanted was to be close to orgasm with him around. She'd rather have the King back.

Again, she was glad to have cracked the window open, knowing the scent of the spring rain would be masking her arousal from filling the room past the herbs.

"Thank you, Etel, do you..." He continued asking his question but the nibble Miels made to her clit cut off all of Etel's rational thought and all she could focus on was how badly she needed to come on him.

His fingers slipped back inside her, but they moved slowly now as he lazily kissed at her cunt, licking when he felt the need.

"Etel?" Sparrow's voice brought her back, a furrow between his brows as he tried to analyze what was happening before him.

"I'm sorry, Master. Could you repeat that?" She tried with all her might to ignore Miels.

"Do you know how long it will take? It is no rush, but I'd like to know when I should send my men to pick up the vials."

"End of next week should be fine. If anything comes up, I'll let you know."

He smiled, though his gaze still searched her for what was going on, as he said, "Thank you. I'll leave you to your work then."

"Thank you, Master."

He was out of the room a second later, his footsteps still discernible in the hall, when Miels's mouth began its onslaught again. He didn't give her a moment this time, just intensified the pleasure he gave her clit and the spots he hit inside her, and had her clutching the table for support, gasping and whimpering out, his name whispered off her tongue with each breath.

Then his free hand slipped up her leg and onto her stomach, pushing down below her navel, and Etel didn't have time to question it before small moans were forced past her lips and she tried not to fall to the ground as her knees gave out.

She came so hard, her arousal coated her legs in puddles, and all she saw were stars. Millions of them, all the color of Miels's dark-green eyes glimmering.

As she came down from her high, Etel realized that her legs

were too wet. There was too much between them, and that's when mortification set in. She glanced at the door to make sure no one came by as she pulled her skirts enough to see Miels. His face was glistening with arousal, and now with the skirts raised, her scent filled the air. There was only so much her herbs or the spring air could mask. She would need to fully open the windows before another member of the Posse decided to make their way into the room.

"Did I just pee on you!" she shrieked, both embarrassed and horrified.

He only laughed, tongue sticking out to lick his face. "You squirted on me, my creature. And I intend on making you do it again tonight."

It took a moment for the meaning to take root in her mind, but when it did, the blush on her skin turned from alarm to desire. She'd heard of squirting, and honestly wasn't all that surprised that she had done so. *That* was the most intense experience of her life.

"Oh," she only mumbled as she stared at his glistening face.

He smirked. "Now drop your skirts before someone comes in and sees you. I don't necessarily *want* to kill any of the palace residents."

She bit her lip to stop the smile from growing as she dropped her skirts.

A moment later, he wiggled out from beneath the table and reached for a small cloth at the edge of the room by the tapped water basin. Most of the water basins didn't have taps—mostly only being used for the showers—but as the Remedies Expert, hers did.

Miels warmed a towel, then moved for her, dropping to his knees again as he softly cleaned between her thighs and down her legs. Etel paid attention to the door the entire time because he didn't even try to hide his position.

Then he moved back for the basin and warmed the towel again before he cleaned himself as he looked at her through the mirror, eyes glimmering mischievously. "It's a shame I must clean this off. I love your taste. I love the evidence of how much you fancy me on my face."

Etel looked down, the blush on her skin bashful now. She fought a losing battle with the smile on her face as she finally allowed herself to grab the knife and begin cutting. "I hate you."

16

MIELS

Miels knew he was good at keeping secrets, but even he was surprised by the lack of rumors in the weeks since he and Etel began sleeping together. Surprised it hadn't gotten out, though to be fair, most of the servants tried more to not pay attention to Etel rather than to watch her. Especially now that she'd forbade him from visiting her workstation again.

The rain pattered against the windowpane in the dawn air as Miels watched Etel sleep beside him, mesmerized by her beauty. By the fact that he hadn't noticed her before a few weeks ago.

He imagined a life without her, a life where he was still whoring with any woman he pleased and felt completely unsatisfied with the thought. Though he didn't have her yet.

His brothers knew of his activities these couple of weeks, that much had been clear when a week ago Miels went to congratulate Sparrow on his engagement and the Master Assassin made it clear he'd smelled Miels's activities as of late. Tristan's immediate *I knew it* told Miels just how much his brothers had picked up without his notice. Miels himself hadn't realized the scent had been that strong, but then again, Etel had taken a favoring to being fucked against the walls and they normally barely made it past the front door. And his brothers did tend to head to their suites late, so it would make sense for them to pass by Miels's door at just the right times.

He'd come in Etel more times in their short time together than he could remember coming in general during the most active of his whoring months.

So again, he was shocked the others hadn't begun talking. Though still, even Sparrow didn't know it was Etel, so the servants definitely wouldn't.

Miels pushed her hair aside so he could see her completely as she laid on her back, then leaned down to kiss her shoulder softly.

This girl really had him by the fucking balls.

And he couldn't be happier about it.

In the couple of weeks he'd had a taste of her, he'd become addicted to the point where he could understand more clearly Sparrow's instinct to kill him for speaking out about Evony. Miels could imagine killing any man who tried to touch his little creature.

He knew as he watched her dream that he'd never be able to touch another woman. Never be able to think of another woman in anything more than a friendly manner. Never be able to live this life without his little creature by his side.

As he watched her, Miels realized James had been right before, and he had been falling in love. Because he knew as he kissed her shoulder again that he'd arrived at the destination. His heart was solely and utterly Etel's.

And it wasn't because of how much he enjoyed her body, but because of the moments in between when he learned everything imaginable about the little expert. Learning how she'd come across remedies—the time she got to spend with her father, and now the memories it brought along—the fact that she was afraid of dogs—irrational and even she didn't understand it—and why she didn't defend herself against the other servants—she felt guilty. Completely undeservedly since she was worth more than she had.

Part of Miels knew it was because Etel, like those of his Posse, didn't stoop so low as to the jabs others tried to throw their way. It was another factor that solidified to Miels that she was perfect for their group. She'd perfectly fall into his family.

She shuffled in her sleep and Miels could tell she was close to waking, so he kissed her twice again, then pulled back to watch those beautiful eyes flutter open.

"Good morning." He grinned at her.

"Morning," she mumbled in her grogginess.

"You look in need of a ravishing, little creature."

A laugh blew out of her nose as she closed her eyes again, turning to her side to snuggle into his chest. "I think you ravished me enough last night."

An amused growl left Miels as his hand fell over her waist and his fingers played at her back. "There can never be enough."

Her smile was sweet as she peeled her eyes open. "Why do you call me your little creature?"

"Because you're mine." The growl was more possessive now.

She rolled her eyes, but her grin grew wider. "And I'm little, I know. I meant why do you call me creature?"

"Because you're as fearsome as a creature. I knew it the moment I met you."

Her gaze narrowed. "Should I be offended?"

He laughed. "You're quiet and hide yourself, make yourself

look fragile. The best and most dangerous of creatures do the same."

A brow quirked this time. "Most dangerous?"

His nose brushed hers softly. "I have no doubt, my love, that if and when it's needed, you'll be a fearsome thing to behold. Defend yourself and anyone you love, show everyone that you are not weak, hold your skills above all else. Like all of the most dangerous creatures, you allow people to think you weak before tearing them to shreds."

She shook her head. "You think too highly of me, spy. Or you've made a woman in me that I am not, one that you imagine. I have none of those qualities."

He kissed her forehead. "You just don't know it yet, haven't had to use that ferocious part of you."

When he met her gaze, she didn't break, but she still sounded unconvinced when she said, "Whatever you say."

He chuckled and hugged her into his chest, the sound of the rain hitting the windows as the sun began to come awake filling the space.

She pushed away. "Let go, Miels. I have to leave before the wing fills."

He shook his head and made sure she couldn't break out of his hold. "Don't leave. Stay with me. Always."

She froze. "What?"

He watched her closely as he said, "Move into my suite, Etel. Keep your workshop, but live here."

"I-I can't do that." She sounded panicked.

"Why not?"

"How exactly would the rumors not spread then?"

He sighed deeply. "Who cares about the rumors!"

"I do!" She pushed away and as much as he didn't want to allow it, he released her as she sat up, the sheet falling off her delectable breasts before she caught it. "Some of the servants might hate me, but the others around the palace respect me. I cannot lose that because everyone thinks I got to where I am by sleeping with you!"

He sat up too. "They won't." He stopped her before she could interrupt. "You know how I know? Because they've seen your work. They see it every day. They know no one knows remedies in this palace like you do, know you're the one to go to if they need anything. Trust me when I say, some servants will spread rumors, as I'm sure they're already trying to, about you out of envy. The others admire your work."

"Why do you even want this, Miels? It's not like you haven't *had* me every day. Like I haven't stayed with you every night," she argued.

His sigh was edged with irritation. "Maybe because I want you to stay in bed rather than run out early every morning. Maybe because I don't want you scared every time you think someone will see or hear us. Maybe because I want to walk you to breakfast the way Spar walks Evony." He pushed out of bed, unashamed as she flushed at his naked, and still somehow aroused, state. "Or maybe it's because I've fallen in love with you, and I want to have you with me always, Etel. I want everyone to know what you are to me."

Her eyes widened and she breathed slowly. "That's not possible."

He scoffed. "That I'm able to love?"

"That you would ever choose me."

"Would you not choose me?"

"I...of c...Miels." She pushed out of bed and threw on the dress that lay discarded on the floor, then turned to him. "Miels, you don't mean that. You'll find a woman deserving of your status, and you'll laugh of ever saying such a thing to me."

Miels's heart beat frantically, but it wasn't in fear that she'd reject him. It was worse somehow. It was the fear that she truly believed him above her. Believed she didn't deserve him.

"Etel." He cradled her face, "If anyone is undeserving of attentions, it is I. You are more than anything I could've imagined. And I can promise you, I will never want another."

She shook her head vigorously as she pulled away. "Miels... I can't. I..."

Miels's jaw ground together as he tried to hold himself still, the way his heart beat mixing with the pain of the rejection. Especially since he knew she felt similarly, even if she wasn't yet in love. She only did this because of her fears. Not of what the others will say because Miels knew deep down, she didn't care about those.

It was the fears she held herself. The ones that told her she wasn't allowed this life, wasn't allowed him.

"I'm in love with you, Etel. I am now, and I will be when you're ready to accept it."

Her eyes brimmed with a shine as she looked down to the mess they'd made on the floor in their rush to be together before meeting his gaze a final time. "I'm sorry, my big creature."

Miels's heart beat uncontrollably at hearing her new nickname for him. Then crumpled to the floor as he watched her walk away.

17

ETEL

Atiana watched her carefully as the tailor's assistant helped her into a cloaked coat in front of the mirror in her suite. Etel loved that she got to be alone in the tailor's suite rather than the main room for fittings. She hated when peers she once worked with watched her try new, and nicer, clothing.

But Etel wasn't entirely sure she loved that this gave Atiana free rein to speak with her without the fear of being overheard. Because Atiana could see something was bothering her. Etel was sure everyone could see it.

"Why exactly do I need this coat now? We are moving into summer, Atiana." Etel tried to distract the girl before she could pry into Etel's sadness.

It felt comfortable being in the presence of a true peer, someone who was on the same level of where Etel now was as the Remedies Expert.

Atiana gave her that smile that said she knew exactly what was happening. "We all need a coat. In the colder months, we will be more occupied, so I would rather finish this for you while I have the time."

Etel didn't argue with the girl as she stuck more pins into the coat to figure out the sizing for Etel's smaller frame.

After a few silent moments, Atiana said, "Would you like to talk about it, Etel?"

She could act like she didn't know what the tailor was speaking of, but Etel didn't have the energy for that. "You've been here a long time, Atiana. Is there no one that you want to be with? That brightens a smile on your face and makes your heart race? That you're so hopelessly in love with you fear being with him will make all your accomplishments null? That being with him will make it seem like your cunt is the only way you got to your position in life?"

Sadness filled Atiana's eyes, but she met Etel's gaze in the mirror as she said, "I do."

For some reason, Etel wasn't expecting that answer. She wondered who. "Then you understand me."

Her eyes were still sad as her lips lifted to a small smile. "I believe you'll have to explain it to me still, Etel. I have lost you."

"All this work you put into your career to have it washed away because you're 'sleeping with a man in a higher position.' We cannot risk that, Atiana!"

Atiana chuckled now. "Oh, Etel, I most certainly do not understand you then."

"What?"

That sad smile again. "I said I loved him. That there is a fear of what would happen of my reputation and career if I were with him, the rumors. But I never once said I would not take every single one of those risks to experience even the slightest moments with him."

Etel's brows furrowed. "Then why are you not with him?"

"It is a lot easier to be with someone who wants you too."

Etel's heart stopped at the thought of Miels not wanting her. She'd imagined it a million times before but now every time she tried, the sadness in his eyes as she walked away came up instead. His voice as he told her he was in love with her came up. His smiles every time they were together, either intimately or just talking, came up.

"I'm sorry," Etel whispered to one of the only women at the palace she believed she could be friends with. One of the only women who seemed like she would like to be friends with Etel. True friends. The other being Gemma if the girl stuck to her promise of taking remedy lessons.

Atiana moved around her so she faced Etel before she said, "Don't be, Etel. The only thing you can have to apologize about is not taking the risk yourself."

"And what of the rumors?"

"And what of your happiness?" Atiana countered without hesitation. "Miels's happiness?"

Etel's eyes bulged, and Atiana laughed. "I did not need Stell to try to send around the gossip mills to know it, Etel. Miels came in for a fitting and the entire time spoke of making calming serums and pregnancy concoctions." She smirked. "Interesting things to teach him, Expert."

Etel laughed. "The calming was because we needed more. He insisted on learning the pregnancy one."

Atiana watched her with a shine to her eyes, like she was happy to see Etel like this. "And you glow when you speak of him."

Etel sighed. "I'm in love with him."

"And he with you?"

She shrugged. "He said so yesterday. Before I left him."

Atiana was only a few years older than Etel, but she seemed so much wiser as she took Etel's cheek in her hand.

"Do not let your fears ruin your future, Etel. That man loves you. And if I had to guess, would immediately stop the pregnancy concoction if you allowed him the chance to showcase his feelings to the whole of the world."

Etel's voice was soft, low, as she said, "He said he wants everyone to know that he's mine."

"And imagine how cute your children would be alongside the Master's."

Etel rolled her eyes. "No children right now. Miels respects that."

Atiana's smile was wider now. "You cannot even say his name without smiling past your eyes."

A blush filled Etel's cheeks. "Weren't you working on this coat?"

Atiana laughed as she moved around Etel to the back once more. It gave Etel the chance to look at the girl through the mirror.

She was beautiful, exceedingly so. Long, dark brown hair. Light brown eyes. A light tan over her skin that matched so perfectly with her hair and eyes. Perfectly shaped eyebrows and long lashes. Taller than the average woman around the palace, she was probably the most beautiful help in the palace.

And yet, whoever she loved didn't reciprocate the feeling. It felt wrong.

Etel wanted to know who the man was. Not to gossip, but so she could beat him for being so blind.

"Thank you, Atiana," she said warmly. "For being a friend."

The tailor only winked at her through the mirror.

~

It was much later than she was normally out of her rooms. Even the nights she had spent with Miels, Etel had never left her suite at such an ungodly hour. She'd always been in his room before midnight.

But it was well past midnight, closer to dawn, as Etel moved for the King's wing.

Etel was only a few steps into the hall that led to the suites of all the King's Posse when the emergency alarms banged through the palace and her heart froze. Those alarms specifically meant that there was an attack on the palace.

And an attack on the palace meant Miels would be in the line of trouble.

In the moments it took for her to come to terms with that, Miels's door opened as he stumbled out, shirt in hand to throw on, eyes bulged in desperation.

Then he saw her and stopped. Sighed so deep, breath left Etel as she watched him relax. "Thank the lords," he muttered as he brought her into his embrace and pushed her into his room.

He didn't release her for a few long seconds as the alarms blared through the palace. Then he kissed her and though they had broken up the day before, Etel would not push him away. She was already terrified to have him leave to deal with this attack.

"I have to go. Please stay here. Stay safe for me," he muttered against her lips as she nodded her assurance, then he kissed her hard. "I love you," he whispered before pulling away and throwing his shirt on.

He was gone before she could say anything back.

Etel felt numb as she walked backward until her knees hit the couch and she fell into it, her gaze never leaving the door he'd walked out of.

Then a second later, it opened and her heart stammered before she saw Miels push the Princess into the room and shut it again, barking out a "There're daggers in the drawer. Take them!"

Princess Rosaelia caught her gaze and swallowed awkwardly. Etel had to assume the Princess could guess what she was doing in there. Etel didn't know what to say to her. She was aware, like most, that the Princess had a crush on the blonde spy.

She knew she should be more formal, but Etel couldn't find it in herself to care at the moment. So she pulled on the drawer beside the couch to pull out two daggers and silently handed one to the Princess.

Rosaelia took it and softly mumbled, "Thank you."

They sat next to one another silently for what felt like ages but was only a few minutes. Then Rosaelia mumbled, "I suspect he does not see you as a sister too?"

Etel's cheeks burned as she turned to the Princess, and the memory of her first time with the spy in the spot the Princess now sat came to her. But she didn't know how to answer.

"As long as he is happy, I am happy," Rosaelia said. "As long as all four of the men in my life are happy, I am happy."

Etel nodded but still couldn't say anything.

Rosaelia got to her feet and moved for the door. "And as long as they are all safe."

She left without waiting for Etel.

But Etel stayed in her spot. Didn't want to leave this suite. Not because she was scared for the attack, but because she had promised Miels she would stay here, and there was so much he was hurting for at the moment, fearing for her safety wouldn't be added to the list.

She stayed sitting there for long moments before she moved for the door to the right that would lead to his room.

She'd stayed in it so many times the past couple of weeks, her body instantly settled when she stepped within, like it recognized she was in Miels's space now and she would be safe.

She moved for the dresser that held his clothes and pulled out his favorite dark green shirt that matched his eyes. It was her favorite one too.

She numbly slipped off her dress, her mind too scattered with the possibility of Miels getting injured to pay too close attention to anything else going on. Then she pulled the shirt over her naked body and moved for the bed.

Pulling the covers back, Miels's scent invaded her senses, and she was soaking wet between her thighs. He always did that to her, even in moments like this where she should be more focused on other matters—like his safety.

She slipped into the bed as the alarms rang for the end of the attack, a lighter baritone now. The entire attack had taken a little over an hour, and every second of it had been anguish to Etel. She was only glad for the Master Assassin and Master Magician's presences. She knew without them, this attack could've lasted hours still.

Etel slipped into the bed as the sun shined through the crack in the curtains and the new day truly began. She knew she should go back to her suite and make some remedies, but she was so exhausted from two nights of restlessness that she couldn't get her body to move even if she desperately needed to. She was finally in the space she felt best in.

Though restlessness still followed her at not knowing whether the only person she loved in this world was safe.

18

ETEL

She'd fallen asleep in his bed.

In only the couple of short weeks she'd shared his bed, she'd become accustomed. The one night she hadn't been there, her body had noticed immediately. Known that his warmth was nowhere around, his scent not holding her. Apparently those short weeks had been enough to teach her body that she could no longer sleep alone. Not comfortably at least.

And though she knew he'd be with the Posse cleaning up the mess of the aftermath of such an attack, Etel had remained restless that morning as she tried to sleep in his bed. Only hopeful that nothing had happened to him.

When, hours later, she felt his lips press against her forehead, she'd fully relaxed into the bed. Even though he hadn't slipped into it beside her. Etel knew he'd only come to check on her before heading back out to deal with the mess of the palace. But simply being in his bed and knowing he was safe had lulled her to such peaceful dreams she'd had to force herself out late that night before he came back.

She'd needed to help the palace with the clean up, see if there were any remedies required from her.

Etel worked through the night, mostly making more concoctions and serums, before moving to the kitchens for breakfast in the morning and finding her way to the alcove she'd been watching through as the two Masters had married.

She was lost in thoughts of marriages and a certain blonde when she heard a shuffling come from behind her. She froze because she knew she was meant to be alone, knew no one else ever ventured to that alcove.

She imagined it the other servants, the ones who hated her, but she couldn't see why they would take the time to torment her when the entire palace was busy with the clean up. As cruel as they were to her, they were still good servants and wouldn't slack off just to tease her.

So, in the seconds it took Etel to turn to the sound and her eyes to widen, she didn't have time to consider an alternative.

But the answer was quite clear—another rebel.

They were supposed to be completely taken care of, but if this one had found this little nook and hidden during the fight and the palace searches, then he'd be fine.

And in a desperate need to leave undetected.

And she'd just detected him.

She pressed her back into the pillars behind her as their eyes met, and she read in his that he did not plan on allowing her out alive. Even she had to internally scoff as the image of Miels crashed into the forefront of her mind.

But she wouldn't berate herself for her feelings for the man. Wouldn't take away the chance for him to be the last thing she thought of.

Then the rebel was coming at her, and instead of waiting to be killed, Etel moved on instinct, her small frame dancing out of his way before he could detect it. Then she swung her arm and put as much might as she could manage into her foot as she kicked the man's back. She did so thrice more in quick succession, so he hardly had time to turn before he was falling back and hitting his head into the pillars.

Her heart raced with the very real possibility that the kicks were not enough and he might turn on her then. But as she turned him and saw his eyes closed, Etel didn't consider anything as she grabbed for the cloth belt around her dress—used mostly for design—and tied it around the man's hands, pulling them up high to wrap around the pillar as quickly as she could.

She didn't have a great many skills, but when she was a child, she'd helped tie so many ropes that she was as great as a seaman in the matter. This rebel would not be going anywhere.

Not that he could at the moment, knocked out as he was.

Etel didn't check his head for any bad injuries. She could tell he was breathing and if he was breathing, then he could talk, could tell the Posse anything they needed to know.

And even if he didn't—couldn't—she needed to tell Miels. She needed to get to him.

Etel didn't think of it before darting out of the small nook and down the corridors, passing hall after hall before making it to the dining hall where she knew the Posse would be readying for breakfast.

She didn't even stop to think of propriety as she slammed open the hall doors and heard them bang back against the walls. Her gaze was utterly and wholly on Miels's spot as he jumped out of his seat at the sight of her.

She raised her hand to stay him before dropping at the waist to catch her breath.

Lords, maybe she needed to join in some training, at least for the runs. Her body needed to increase its stamina because she hadn't run long at all to get to this hall, and she was completely out of breath.

When she caught her breath enough to speak, her gaze landed back on Miels as she huffed with each statement. "Rebel. In the hall. Tried attacking."

Her breath returned to a more normal state as she picked herself back up to see the others on their feet, awaiting her. And again, her gaze gravitated to Miels.

He moved to her. They all did, but Etel could tell he moved to her for another purpose.

So she glared his way, making sure he understood not to touch her. Not to try anything. No matter how much she wanted him to.

She turned as the others came close and led them to her private nook. The Master Assassin growled at the guards to recheck the palace, something that made Etel feel for the guards. It wasn't entirely their fault to have missed this one, though she understood that they were trained to catch everyone.

When they turned the corner, she stopped by her window and watched the Posse fill into the small space, Miels always beside her. Feeling his undivided gaze on her the entire walk had been like being on fire, the heat far too enticing to be safe.

Etel wanted to pay attention as Sparrow kicked the man, but her every morsel was alive with being so close to Miels again. She wanted nothing more than to push him against the walls and allow him to have his way with her.

She was broken from her daydream when Miels's body covered her before the rebel, his voice hard and possessive as he said, "I believe in cases like these, we are the ones asking questions."

Now with Miels standing less than a foot in front of her, all

Etel had to do was lean forward and she'd be touching him again. She'd feel his warmth envelop her. She'd be safe.

It was torture forcing herself to remain still as they spoke to the man, then had two guards peel him away to the dungeons.

Miels's hard gaze was on her for long moments before they were all racing down the corridors. Like a gravitational pull, Etel followed Miels to the large doors that led to the stables.

And stopped there.

She watched as the entire group headed for the horses, watched as Miels himself readied a horse. Watched and hated herself for not going after him, for not running into his arms and kissing him lest he were to get hurt running off to whatever Queen they were fighting.

She hated herself for how much she loved him, yet still wouldn't do a thing about it.

19
MIELS

I know you would prefer to—need to—remain by her *side.*

Miels couldn't argue with Sparrow there because as much as he wanted to go after Evony—his newest and most beloved of sisters—and the horny couple, he needed to be by Etel's side. Especially so soon after an attack. He couldn't risk anything happening while he was away and Etel possibly getting hurt in the interim.

So he caught her stare from across the greens and knew she understood that he would be staying. He couldn't tell if she was relieved or upset with the news.

She turned back for the palace before he could decipher it and he had to breathe deeply to keep from running after her and demanding she talk to him. Instead, he turned to the others and watched them ride off, hoping the search for the three Southerners wouldn't take long and they'd all return safely.

As much as he wanted to stay by Etel's side, Miels also hated that he couldn't be with his family to keep them safe.

Edmund turned to him when the group was out of sight, his eyes dull with guilt. "How did he convince you to stay?"

Miels gave one of his conceited smirks. "You're as much a father to me as you are to him, Ed. Gotta make sure you're safe."

He rolled his eyes. "As your father, you little jackass, I know when you're not telling me something."

Miels winked and threw his arm around the King's shoulders, knowing he was joking only to hide the pain of what he'd caused with his second daughter. He needed to remain strong as the King, but Miels could see the pain in his eyes like only his Posse could. "Then why don't you try and figure it out."

Edmund sighed. "You kids will be the death of me."

Miels shrugged as he led the King inside. "You have two heirs to take your place. And one of them is married to my brother, so I have no worries about my status."

Ed laughed. "And the other fancies you. Did you forget about that part? You could take my place in that route."

Miels rolled his eyes because he hated thinking that Ro, who he looked to as a sister, actually fancied him. Especially now that he could only picture Etel in his mind's eye. "I would never touch Ro like that, my king."

Edmund clasped Miels's shoulder. "That is why I like you."

They laughed as they strolled down the corridor toward the stairs.

"Where're we going?" Miels asked.

"I asked the Remedies Expert to make me some shots for my gut health."

Miels forced himself not to freeze up at the mention of Etel, and the memory of Edmund walking into Etel's workstation to ask for that gut shot while he was between her legs underneath the table.

"I need to pick them up." Edmund stopped before him.

"And you do not have to follow me around like a lost pup."

Miels clasped his shoulder in a friendly shake. "Don't be ridiculous, Ed. The others are gone. Who else will I follow around like a lost pup?"

Again, Edmund rolled his eyes and continued on toward Etel's suite.

Miels prepared himself as they walked together to see Etel in the presence of one of his Posse. He needed to keep his reactions controlled since Etel still wasn't sure about them, still didn't want their relationship known.

If there even was a relationship any longer.

She'd gone to him before the attack. She'd been in the hall, only steps away from his door, when the alarms had blared through the palace. He'd been so scared he wouldn't make it to her suite in time, he'd rushed out faster than any of the others.

And been so relieved to see her at his door.

He'd wondered later, after the attack, what she'd been doing there. Known she'd been there to see him but needing to know why.

Then he'd been too relieved to go back to his suite and find her in his bed. Scared at first that she had left when he didn't see her in the common area, then elated when he found her sleeping in his bed. He'd needed to kiss her forehead for his own sanity and had loved the way she had mumbled his name and fallen into a deep sleep.

When he'd returned late that night after dealing with affairs, and she'd been gone, he'd known she wasn't yet ready for their relationship. He'd been upset, but thankful that, at least for the attack, she had been safe in his suite. In his bed.

When he and Edmund entered her workstation, Etel's breath caught as their eyes met before hers darted away. She gave a slight bow of the head to Edmund and was her natural soft and sweet self as she handed him the remedies and gave him a bit of information regarding each one, having added more than just gut shots.

The fact that she wouldn't even look his way pierced his heart stronger than anything else could've.

Trying to focus on the King, the palace, the politics of royalty hadn't distracted Miels nearly as much as he'd desired in the time his friends were gone. Because every other breath he took brought Etel back into his thoughts, only divided by his worry for his family, new and old. Waiting for them to return was another type of pain.

But that one had been easily brushed aside when Evony's crude voice in his head made him jump before he rushed to the stables to meet up with them. As they all blew into the palace for their baths and the preparations of dinner, he'd smiled genuinely for the first time in too many long days.

Miels enjoyed their company, but having them back had only blocked the pain of not having Etel for a short period. By the time they were sitting to eat, the Remedies Expert was entirely taking over his thoughts once more.

And as his best friends, Sparrow and Tristan noticed imme-diately. James too, though he raised his brows as if to say *I know, love is tough.*

He even felt it from the girls, though they did a better job at concealing that they were curious about his relationship. Miels knew that Evony knew because of her big-mouthed husband, but even said big-mouthed husband didn't know what he was going through. He knew they were all equally curious and attempting to give him his privacy.

He laughed to himself at how horribly their little Posse worked these matters.

20

ETEL

Knocks on her door only came this late in an emergency, so Etel rushed to the door to her suite door and yanked it open.

To find Tristan on the other side.

And immediately her heart sank to her feet at the thought of anything happening to Miels.

"What's happened?" She sounded breathless, but she couldn't control herself at the thought of him hurt, tears already springing to her eyes.

A small smirk quirked the man's lips. "Calm down. Miels is fine."

She sighed her relief, then her heart stopped as she processed what he'd said. "He told you about us?"

"No." Tristan stepped into Etel's workstation, forcing her to move back, and closed the door behind him. "But he's my brother and I'm a trained spy. I could figure something was off about him. But the way he looked at you, reacted to you when you stopped that rebel, was what really gave it away."

"Oh." She kept moving back until her legs hit the couch at the far corner of her workstation, and she fell into it.

"If there is an 'us,' then why is he hurting so much, Etel?" He followed her and took the seat beside her.

She studied him, for once not as her superior but as her lover's brother. "Why are you here, Tristan?"

"To find out why the woman my brother is in love with isn't in his bed at the moment. Why she hasn't taken over his entire suite by now. I cannot imagine Miels ever wanting you to leave."

Her gaze dropped to her hands in her lap. "He didn't."

He let out a breathy laugh. "Oh, I know." When she met his gaze, he asked, "So why aren't you there?"

"He asked me to move into his suite." She stared blankly at him, and though he and Miels were meant to look as similar as Evony and Rosaelia, like Sparrow to the Princess, Etel had never been able to feel anything for Tristan.

"Is that meant to explain why you aren't there, Etel?"

She shrugged. "The reason he never told you is because I didn't want anyone finding out. So when he asked me, I said no because there would be no way the whole palace wouldn't know by lunch if I moved in."

"Don't you love him?"

Etel met Tristan's warm and nonjudgemental gaze and could feel how sad hers looked to him. "Before he even knew of my existence."

He gave her a small grin. "I think his ego would inflate a little too much if he knew that."

"I didn't tell him." Sadness overtook her as she thought about it, her gaze landing on the spot he'd been standing when he'd come to her with the original offer to keep them secret. "When he told me he loved me, I didn't say it back."

"Why not?" he asked softly.

Etel couldn't break her gaze from the spot by the workstation table. "I wouldn't have been able to leave if I'd said it. I barely kept myself strong enough to walk out as it was."

Another breathy laugh. "Yes, your strength. It's quite the impressive beast."

Her gaze finally snapped over, the reminder of Miels's reasoning behind calling her creature bubbling up. "What?"

"The way you knocked that rebel down. Someone as small as you. I'd be keen to know how you did it."

She shrugged like what she'd done wasn't impressive even though she herself thought it was a little too impressive. "I... watch you guys. When you train. Small as I am, I can hide without you noticing."

He smirked wickedly.

"Well," she corrected. "I watch Miels. It's like my brain memorizes his every movement and when I get back here, at nights when no one needs me, I bring it all to the front of my mind and try to mimic everything Miels did. It was so hard at first, I thought myself ridiculous for even attempting any of it, but I couldn't get myself to stop. It was like my heart had come up with the perfect excuse to get me to continue ogling Miels —I needed to see what he was doing in order to learn. After a few months though, I actually got quite good. Then I made myself a bag to hit and kick and started practicing those. I honestly didn't think I would actually be any good in a fight, especially not with anyone trained. But I think my size kinda helps me get away. And the fact that people don't expect it from me."

Tristan leaned close and pressed his forehead into hers, and somehow, Etel could tell it was a brotherly gesture. "If you tell Miels that, I don't care how good you think your pregnancy tonics are, you'll fall with child immediately."

Etel laughed and pushed him away.

She grew serious after a moment as she watched Tristan and brought up the similarities he had with his best friend. He was a true brother to Miels in all ways but blood, and Etel could see a future where her child ran into Uncle Tristan's arms. "I hate that I'm hurting him. I'm in love with him."

"Then why not tell him?"

She analyzed Tristan. "I'm scared this isn't what he really wants. He's so far above me. What if he only thinks it's what he wants because he's finally learning what a heart is?"

Tristan laughed at the jab she'd made at his friend's expense. Then he caught her gaze with a hold that didn't allow her to break and there was so much certainty there. "He won't change his mind. Hell, he wouldn't be able to if he tried. When Miels gives his heart to something, he gives it all. And with you, that's a more literal statement." He pushed her softly. "And he's most definitely not above you, sweetheart."

A small smile grew on her lips as she imagined Miels walking down the corridors, training with the guards, laughing with Sparrow and Tristan. As she imagined him laughing at something she'd said, telling her secrets that weren't allowed out of the Posse, in the heated moments that she knew even the numerous women before her hadn't experienced.

Tristan stood to his feet and held out a hand to her. "Let me take you to him."

It was like an instant click in her because Etel didn't even think about it as she placed her hand in his and got to her feet.

He released her hand when they got to the corridors and she knew it was because rumors were one thing, but the last thing they needed was anyone thinking anything was going on between the two of them. Only after her relationship with Miels was public could she hold Tristan and everybody know it was a brotherly gesture. His wink told her that much.

When they got to Miels's door, a sense of coming home settled into Etel's chest.

Tristan pulled her behind him, so his far larger frame completely blocked her from view, then knocked on the door.

Though she could barely see through the space between Tristan's arm and chest, she could tell Miels was his usual shirtless self when he opened the door.

His voice was pained as he looked to his best friend. "What do you want?"

"Aren't we grouchy tonight?" Tristan said in a mocking manner.

"Tristan," he growled.

"What're you doing, brother?"

Etel couldn't tell where Tristan was going with this.

"I'm not going out whoring if that's why you're here." Etel froze. "Pretend I'm Sparrow. That'll never be an option for me again."

Tristan chuckled and shuffled over as he muttered, "I know."

Etel caught on to Tristan's antics a moment before her gaze locked with Miels's—he was proving to her that Miels's words weren't prettily made for her, but ones he meant. He would never touch another woman again.

Miels's gaze shot between the two of them before stopping on Etel as he took a step forward, then stopped himself as if he expected her to push him away.

Etel could only stare. She missed staring up into those gorgeous dark-green orbs.

Then Tristan interrupted with a laugh as he headed for his room a few feet behind Etel, directly across from them. "I would tell you two to keep it down, but considering I haven't heard you once yet, I'd assume you don't need the reminder."

When Tristan disappeared, Miels's gaze narrowed, and she could see the hope blistering. "Etel?"

She stepped forward and took his face between her hands, bringing him down so their foreheads touched. "I want to move in so bad, I've already decided where I'm moving your table. And what color to change your curtains to."

A close-lipped laugh passed him, the hope growing in his eyes as he whispered, "Ours."

"What?"

"It's our table. Our curtains." He hesitated. "If you say yes."

"I'm in love with you, Miels. I have been since the first time I saw you, and I don't care about anything else anymore. I want you. I want us. I need it."

His eyes brimmed with tears. His arms wrapped around her waist and hauled her off her feet as he kissed her hard.

He kicked the door closed behind him and pushed her against it. "I think I need to teach you a lesson for putting me through so much pain."

She laughed against his lips. "Please." He kissed her hard. "I need to learn my lesson, Miels. Punish me."

He growled and ripped her dress open in one swipe.

EPILOGUE
MIELS

"Fuck, Etel. I told you, you were a dangerous creature." He pounded into her harder, relishing the feeling of her tight pussy clenching around his cock. "This fucking cunt is going to make me come prematurely."

She laughed into his shoulder. "If you come, baby, what will that say about your whoring past?"

"It'll say no woman has ever been so good for me as you are," he grunted as he pressed his lips back to hers.

Their tongues fought for dominance as his hands slipped beneath her skirts to take handfuls of her ass, fingers skimming the edge of her crack. He loved the sounds she made when he went near her forbidden little hole, loved the way she clenched extra hard around his cock and scratched down his back when he did so.

Before his tongue could win out, a shocked gasp came from their side and Miels froze, buried deep inside his creature.

He turned to find Princess Rosaelia standing at the door, eyes wide as saucers as she looked between the two of them and down to the jumble of mess their clothes made between them. In their haste to come together, they hadn't bothered to undress, rather pushing her dress up and his trousers to his knees.

In this moment, he was glad for it. It was bad enough that Ro caught them, but he didn't need her catching a more revealing eyeful.

Rosaelia stuttered, muttered an apology, and raced out of the room.

Miels caught Etel's mortified look as he pulled out of her and began pulling at his trousers.

"Miels, you have to go after her…"

"I know." He hurried to the door before Rosaelia was lost in the maze of the palace, tying his trousers and attempting to settle his shirt back into place.

They had been in a small room on the third floor, so far off that fabrics covered furniture and a light settling of dust sat about the room. No one knew of these rooms. Miels hardly even knew of them before Etel had dragged him in there.

Miels caught the end of Rosaelia's dress turning the corner and followed her out of the corridor and onto the balcony. She stopped at the edge and took a large breath.

"Ro," he called, staying by the palace doors to give her space.

She jumped and turned to him. "Miels. I am so sorry. I heard sounds, and I guess I was too distracted, and my mind wasn't putting two and two together…I'm sor—"

"Ro," he interrupted. "Don't apologize. I'm only sorry *you* were the one that had to see us."

She looked offended. "Because I'm the innocent, naive little Princess?"

A smirk turned Miels's lips without his permission. He couldn't help finding amusement in the fact that's what she was offended by. "No, Ro. Because of your feelings." *For me.*

Her breath caught, and her eyes widened again. "Miels, I..." She shook her head. "I *did* fancy you. For a while. But these past few weeks, I've found myself less and less drawn to you. No offense, of course." She threw in the last part hastily as he quirked a brow.

Miels laughed. "If you are being honest, Ro, then trust me, I am not offended."

"I am," she insisted. "When I officially heard of your relationship with Etel—that you'd fallen in love—I was honestly so happy for you, Miels. I'd suspected after seeing her in your suite the night of the attack, but when she moved into your suite, I was ecstatic. Now two of my men are in love. But honestly, that's when I knew my feelings were completely gone."

Now his lips twitched up in a soft smile. "Thank you, Ro. I truly adore having you as my Princess and my sister. Know that I would never want to jeopardize that."

"I love it too, Miels. And I love you. Just not romantically." He laughed with her as her eyes darted behind him, and Miels knew without turning that Etel had stopped by the doors. "But as your Princess, I must declare that you shall never leave your woman unsatisfied. A reformed whore such as yourself should know as much."

He laughed harder now and could hear Etel's soft giggles behind him.

Rosaelia stepped up and cupped his cheek as she stared up at him. "You're a good man, Miels, and I am lucky to call you one of my closest friends. I am excited for the happiness Etel will bring to your life."

Miels stepped closer to wrap his arms around her, but she stopped him.

"As loving of a gesture a hug may be, after catching you two, I'd rather not right now." She ignored his chuckles and rose to the tips of her toes and kissed him lightly on the cheek. "Now get back to your woman."

"Yes, Princess," Miels mocked her as she walked in from the balcony and into the palace, leaving a gentle touch on Etel's arm to let the little expert know her Princess wasn't angry with what she'd walked in on.

Miels waited until the sounds of Rosaelia's feet were no longer detectable, then cockily strolled to his woman. He pushed her a step into the palace and turned so her back hit the door to the balcony. "You heard the Princess. I cannot leave my woman unsatisfied."

She tried to push at him, but did so weakly. "Miels, we're basically on the balcony."

He hiked up her dress as one hand undid his trousers once more. "Yes, maybe I can make you scream now. Let the whole of the greens hear us."

"Miels, no!" She giggled as he once more picked her up and aligned his length to her entrance.

He tsked. "Wrong word."

She looked at him with heady and narrowed eyes. "Miels..." He pumped into her, hard, and saw how shocked even she was as she screamed, "Yes!"

"There we go," he teased against her skin. "Now you've got the right word."

WITH
THE
ICE
CATCHING
TWILIGHT

WITH THE ICE CATCHING TWILIGHT

ROSAELIA

She could still hear him—Miels trying to convince her not to brashly talk of leaving because of his relationship with Etel. He insisted that they would not be so public to rub it in her face.

It made her smile, his desire to keep her around. But not in the way it would've months ago. Now, Rosaelia only saw Miels as a good friend. No more silly crush.

And she truly thought him a perfect match to Etel's quiet nature. Hopefully he believed her because her decisions truly had nothing to do with him or any relationship he found himself in.

As the water rocked around her as she stood on the edge of the ship she'd snuck onto, she could hear the rest of her little family, the Posse they were called. Her childhood brother, Sparrow, and his new wife, Rosaelia's true twin sister, Evony, had thought her ludicrous to want to come to the Island Nation.

Rosaelia knew they'd done it out of love. That they believed her naivety in walking to the local town unprotected still lingered.

But she'd learned since then. Trained, both with the others and by herself. She would never be so weak again.

While she'd learned hand-to-hand combat and the use of daggers, held swords and ran laps, felt the true impact of a spare with the Posse, Rosaelia had taught herself archery.

It had started as a silly challenge when she'd been upset, only moments after leaving her first fitting for training wear after Sparrow had found out about her night out in town. She'd felt so humiliated, so weak, so demure. It was a feeling Rosaelia never wanted to feel again.

So as she'd passed the end of the training yards and her gaze had landed on the bow and arrow, she'd felt the need, deep within, to take the two pieces. She'd run deep enough into the surrounding forest to not be heard while still close enough to go home if needed.

Then she'd set up and shot the arrow away from the palace's direction.

And directly away from her target.

Which only happened after her weak arms had been able to pull at the bow at all.

As Rosaelia watched the water lap as it hit the side of her ship, she laughed. How weak and naive she truly had been.

But no longer.

Now she wore her bow and arrow on her back, in the least impressive of all her dresses so as not to go noticed, and in a cloak of low quality. It was thick enough to keep her warm in the cold nights of the Island Nation she'd only heard of, but nothing compared to what her Princess's cloak would've gotten her.

Her Princess's cloak.

Her Princess's mentality.

Her Princess's naivety.

She would never go back to such stupidity. Never allow herself to be the center of such embarrassment.

And though she was angry with herself for the person she had been, Rosaelia could not find an ounce of herself to be angry with her father, the King. He'd done everything to protect her and give her the life Evony had gone without.

Rosaelia could also not find it in herself to be angry with the men in her life—Sparrow, Tristan, and Miels. They'd all done it out of love as well. Wanted to protect her because of how much they loved her and nothing more. Nothing vindictive about it.

As she thought about the four men she loved more than life itself, a sadness entered her again. For leaving them. For going away with nothing but a note she'd hidden.

Rosaelia had let them think her rash, jumping with the need to come to the Island Nation and find her mother, the past Queen of the Northern Lands who wanted to kill her twin and her father. Who wanted to take from Rosaelia everyone who mattered to her.

But not Rosaelia.

Because she had been no threat to the Queen. Rowena had not found her impressive enough to even entertain stopping. It had been the final thrash of the nail within Rosaelia's heart.

But the Posse believed her soft enough to be angry for her people, to be angry for the Posse, to be angry with her mother, to be angry. But never to do a thing about it.

She could not blame them. In her time believing it was her twin sister who was betraying them, Rosaelia had done nothing about it but go to the four men she loved. Trusted them to take care of matters.

Well, now it was her turn to take care of matters.

While the Posse believed her to be locked away in the

Southwest library she loved to venture to, Rosaelia had gone there only to leave the note within the one book she always pulled out when she was there. Sparrow knew the one.

It would be another week, possibly two if she was lucky, before they didn't hear anything and went looking for her. It would be then that after searching the library and sleeping quarters for her, Sparrow would pull out the book to find the note she'd left behind, the one telling her family how much she loved them and how much responsibility she felt not only to her people in the Northern Lands but the people of the Island Nation to stop her mother.

Rosaelia could already picture how truly angry they would be. How Evony would cloak them to come up to the Island Nation and find her, because Rosaelia had no doubts they would come immediately for her. Which only meant she had about two weeks to take care of this problem. Three if she were lucky.

Hopefully, that would be plenty enough time for her.

Time to protect herself with the archery she'd forced herself to hone in, and while she wasn't yet a professional, Rosaelia knew she was well off enough. And after the tips she'd nondescriptly received from Evony's most favored people, Gemma and James, Rosaelia was sure she'd do just fine.

Time to be off on her own and show the world she was no damsel. Show them that her Princess status meant nothing because she was not feeble. She, who traveled across the oceans on a ship she'd boarded without permission. She, who was running to the enemy—both her mother and the Islanders—and ready to fight. She, who would come out victorious.

Time to bring together the bridge between the Island Nation and Northern Lands. Find a way to take the savage politics of the Islanders and mesh them with the civility of the Northern and Southern Lands.

And most importantly, time to find Queen Rowena and kill her.

Continue the story in
With the Ice Catching Twilight...

JOIN MY AUTHOR NEWSLETTER

~

Sign up for Nelly Alikyan's newsletter to be the first to know about new releases and cover reveals, receive exclusive content —like a special scene or two—and be up to date about any other exciting news, i.e. events, signed copies, etc.

www.nellyalikyan.com

ABOUT THE AUTHOR

～

Nelly Alikyan is a girl from the Los Angeles Valley who's constantly on the move—from Boston to London to wherever she chooses next. She's the only reader in her family—not her only cause as the black sheep—and has dreamt of being a writer for as long as she can remember.

When she's not working on her books or in the real world, she's on Youtube at Nelly Alikyan!

For more books and updates:
www.nellyalikyan.com

ACKNOWLEDGMENTS

~

Firs

CPSIA information can be obtained
at www.ICGtesting.com
Printed in the USA
LVHW110447071022
730138LV00005B/257

9 781956 847055